Tin Hats and
Gas Masks

Tin Hats and Gas Masks

Joan M. Moules

ROBERT HALE · LONDON

© Joan M. Moules 2007
First published in Great Britain 2007

ISBN 978-0-7090-8235-4

Robert Hale Limited
Clerkenwell House
Clerkenwell Green
London EC1R 0HT

2 4 6 8 10 9 7 5 3 1

Typeset in 11½/16pt Palatino
by Derek Doyle & Associates, Shaw Heath
Printed and bound in Great Britain
by Biddles Limited, King's Lynn

For Cara, Angharad, Jack, Becki, Dan.

CHAPTER 1

1939

Johnny felt miserable. The misery had been building up inside him all the way down in the train. Or was it up – did you go up or down to the country from London? He didn't even know the teacher who was travelling with them. She was just 'Miss'. He had seen her before – she took the top class in school, and it was only this morning that he knew his own teacher wasn't coming.

'Miss Power will be travelling with the evacuees,' she said as she marshalled them into the playground. 'Now remember to behave properly, both on the train and when you reach your new homes. I don't suppose it will be for long.'

'Where are we going, miss?' someone asked.

'I don't know, and that's the truth, but you'll be safe there until the war's over.'

His mum was at the station. 'Now you behave yourself

and don't forget to post the card as soon as you get there,' she said, hugging him. 'And put a message on it, tell me if you're all right. I'll be down to see you in a week or two, once you've settled in like.' She clenched her fist and pretended to box him under the chin. 'Don't let us down now,' she said, then she was gone and he didn't really see her go.

Now here he was – in the country. He still didn't know what the place was called, but judging by the length of the journey it was a long, long way from London and home. Billy Green, one of his mates, nudged him.

'Wonder what it'll be like, Johnny?'

'Dunno Billy, but we're here now – ain't nothing we can do about it.'

'Come along children, move up now.' The woman who spoke was tall and fat, and had a booming voice. She had already told them her name was Mrs Poole.

'I'm the billeting officer,' she said, 'and once you are all settled into your places I shall check to see everyone is behaving well.'

There it was again, this emphasis on good behaviour. 'Anyone 'ud think we was a lot of hooligans,' Johnny whispered to Billy, then he concentrated on the scene around him so he could blot out the pictures of home that were snapping away in his head.

Grown-ups were going along the lines of children, but Mrs Poole held them off. 'Just point to the ones you want,' she said.

Johnny turned to Billy again. 'Like a bleedin' cattle market.'

The billeting officer had walked across to a grey-haired lady and gentleman. She consulted the papers she was holding, and after a few moments turned back towards the children.

'Billy Green,' she called. Johnny braced himself. Looked like Billy had been 'chosen'. He hoped they wanted another boy in the same house. But no, the couple were leaving now with Billy, and he didn't even look back. Johnny laughed, and as more children left and went off with their prospective hosts and hostesses he grew noisier till Mrs Poole said, 'You boy, be quiet now. Your turn will come.'

He watched all the others going. His friends from school and many he had never seen before from other London districts. The hall was almost empty now and Johnny panicked.

'P'raps they'll send us back,' he said loudly, 'I didn't want to come here in the first place.'

A girl standing next to him said, 'Sshh, you want to get taken too, don't you? It'll be like a holiday in the country – my mum said so.'

Before Johnny could reply someone claimed her and he knew with sudden clarity that he would be the last one to go. Out of all these kids, hundreds of them it seemed. He laughed even more loudly and watched with pleasure the distaste on some of the adults' faces.

When there were three left, two brothers and himself, he wanted very badly to go to the lavatory. He'd have to hold on, be awful though if he wetted himself here in this strange place.

'How old is he?' they'd say, '*Ten*, almost eleven!' And they'd choose the other two.

Only one lady remained now, and she seemed younger than most of them had been.

'Well, I really only wanted one,' she was saying, standing in front of the three of them, 'but as they're brothers . . . you *will* find them somewhere else if I can't manage, won't you?'

'I'm sure you'll cope,' Mrs Poole's voice was less strident now, 'but of course if it is too much . . . they'll be company for each other and a great help to you. Come along boys,' and she ushered them towards the woman.

'Now young man, what's your name?' She looked at her list.

'Johnny, and I want to be excused.'

'Oh, can't you wai. . . .'

'It's *urgent* miss.'

'All right, there's no need to shout. If you had been less loud earlier on, we would probably have placed you by now. Go on then, through that door and round the corner. And don't be long.'

He cried a bit while he was there, but was in charge of himself again when he returned.

'If nobody wants me I can go home, can't I?' He slung his gasmask round his neck and picked up his suitcase.

'Don't worry, Johnny, somebody'll want you. It's the room mostly, you see. Times like this, houses should be made of elastic so they could stretch to accommodate all the children.'

He nearly did pipe his eye then, and to stop himself he said quickly, 'What do we do then, go round all the

bleedin' streets until we find a bed? I'd rather go home.'

'Don't swear, and come with me.' Suddenly she was brisk again. 'I think I know where there's a spare room.'

Johnny's first impression of the house was of its size and the long path. Like something from the films, he thought, but kept quiet as he walked by Mrs Poole's side to the front door. The lady who opened it looked at him.

'I already have an evacuee,' she said.

'I know, Mrs Dover, but you do have room for more, four bedrooms I believe.'

'One is my husband's study.' She glanced at Johnny again. 'You had better bring the boy in for a moment.'

'Go and sit over there, son,' the lady said to him when they were in what seemed to Johnny to be a very large room – all carpet and very little furniture. Why, at home their living-room was packed with all the things they needed. Not at all like this.

He sank into the depths of the armchair she indicated. It was as soft as his gran's feather-bed that time he had stayed with her when he was a small boy. He'd never forgotten that. Fancy thinking about it now.

Mrs Poole and the lady, who obviously owned the house, had gone to the other end of the room. Although they were speaking quietly and he couldn't hear the exact words, he knew Mrs Poole was trying to get her to take him in. If she's got four bedrooms, or even three, then she'll have to, he thought, because Mrs Poole was the one with the power here. He'd learned that much this afternoon.

Lifting his arms to the sides of the luxurious chair, he expanded his chest. Well, he'd stay for tonight, but tomorrow he'd be off home. Won't bother to unpack, wouldn't be worth it.

They were walking towards him now and Mrs Poole was smiling. 'Johnny, this will be your billet, your new home. You're a very lucky boy to be staying here.' Turning towards the lady she said, 'I'm sure it will work. Probably better than two the same sex, although we do try to place boys with boys of course, but sometimes it simply isn't possible.'

When she had left, Mrs Dover said, not unkindly, 'You had better come upstairs and unpack. Then you can wash and sort yourself out before dinner. We've another evacuee here, Anita Evesham, about your age.'

'We had dinner on the train,' Johnny said, 'some sandwiches.'

'We eat at night here,' she replied.

'Don't you have nothing dinner-time?'

'A snack,' she said over her shoulder as they went upstairs.

She left him in the bedroom, which he was relieved to see wasn't as large as the downstairs room.

'The bathroom is at the end of the landing, it's marked on the door,' she said. 'Come downstairs as soon as you are ready.'

Within seconds of her going there was a tap on the door which was still partly open, and a face with a stream of dark brown hair surrounding it looked round at him.

'I'm Anita Evesham. May I come in?'

'Johnny Bookman,' he said. 'I jest arrived.'

'I know. I was watching from the top of the stairs and saw you. Shall I help you unpack?'

'No,' Johnny said, panic in his voice. 'I mean, I'm not staying. Not after tonight.'

She gazed at him in amazement. 'Not staying, Johnny, but you *have* to.'

'Oh yes. Who says?' He threw his case on to the bed and the tin hat tied to the handle banged against his hand.

Anita giggled. 'What's that?'

'What does it look like, nitwit? It's a tin hat.'

'What do you want that for?'

'For the bombs of course. I don't want me bloody brains blown out, do I?'

'Is that all you've got? That little old suitcase?'

'I told you, I'm not staying long. And this little old suit-case has seen some action in its time. It was me dad's when he went on his fresh-air holidays.'

'Fresh-air holidays? What are they?'

Johnny threw his gasmask case on to the bed with the other one. 'All the kids used to go on 'em when he was a nipper. Week in the country – he's often told me about it. Loved it, he did.'

'We usually go to the seaside for our holidays,' she said.

'Miss La-de-da, ain't you? I saw you on the train,' he added, watching her. 'Where d'you live?'

'In London, but I'm not there much. I go to boarding-school. Well I did, but my school was requisitioned the week before last, so it closed down. I had to go to another one, a council school, and now today I've been evacuated with them and came here.'

Johnny had never seen anyone so calm. 'And don't you mind?' he asked.

She shrugged her shoulders. 'What, coming here? No, not really. Might be a bit of an adventure.'

'Blimey!'

Mrs Dover called up the stairs, 'Anita, Johnny, come downstairs now please.'

'What's she like?' Johnny said.

'Don't really know yet. I had only been here an hour myself when you arrived.'

It seemed a strange evening to Johnny. For a start he wasn't used to eating a full dinner at night. Half-way through he remembered the postcard he had to send to his mum and dad.

'Where's the post office?' he said.

'In the square, Johnny.'

'I'll go and post me card in a minute.' He struggled with the food on his plate.

'Can't do it tonight, don't want you out in the blackout.' Mr Dover spoke for the first time during the meal.

'There's a pillar-box on the corner, Johnny,' Mrs Dover said, 'I'll slip along with it for you after dinner if you really want it in there this evening.'

He mumbled his thanks. 'I can go though.'

Nevertheless it was Mr Dover who eventually took both the children's pre-stamped and addressed cards along to the post-box. Johnny sucked his pencil for a long while before he wrote, *I got here this afternoon. Its posh. Theres a gerl here. Dont know what this citys called. Johnny.*

14

Alone in his bedroom later he felt like crying again. 'Don't be bloody stupid,' he said to himself, 'play yer cards right and you can go home tomorrow.'

The sheets felt cold against his skin which was still tingling from the brisk cold-water wash he had given himself.

'There's plenty of hot water,' Mrs Dover had said. 'Would you like a bath?'

Anita had one but he opted out of that. 'I had one last night, miss,' he said. Anita giggled, and Mrs Dover smiled at him.

'Call me Mrs Dover.'

Actually, he thought, she doesn't seem a bad sort, but as he had no intention of being here for long it didn't really matter what she was like. Trouble was, he'd need money for the journey back. He could slip out of the house and find his way to the bus or rail station, and he had two ten-shilling notes, one from his mum and one from his dad. He grinned at the thought that neither knew the other had given him money!

Then there were his sixpences and threepenny-bits. He'd been saving them up to buy a bike, and he'd brought his hoard with him, it was in a cocoa-tin in his case. He had no idea what the fare would be from here, but he didn't want to spend it all.

He wondered if they could send him back. P'raps he'd better not go home straight away. Go missing for a while, then when he turned up on his mum's doorstep she'd be so glad to see him she'd let him stay. The picture of his mum at the railway station, was it really only this morning, would not go away. He supposed she had gone so quickly because she didn't want to cry, but then she didn't have to send him away, did she? No one could make her.

He got out of bed and went along to the bathroom again. There was a light on the landing, it had been left switched on and a heavy black curtain was pulled across the window there. Anita's bedroom door was ajar and he could see the end of the bed and the back of a chair with her clothes hanging across. There was no sound coming from the room and he thought she must be asleep.

The bathroom was cold. There was an enormous white bath along one side and a small white washbasin next to it. On the wall next to the lavatory were three large ducks which looked as though they were chasing each other to the door. The lavatory was much lower than theirs at home and he could only just reach the chain by standing on tiptoe. He stifled the urge to jump up to it because it was so quiet here, but when he pulled it the noise crashed around him and he scuttled quickly back to the bedroom.

Back in bed he felt tears pricking in his eyes. 'Stupid nit,' he said, 'lots of kids are in strange beds tonight. All those hundreds who were on the train, and *thousands* of others too, all over the country.'

Some of the little ones had cried on the train, he remembered; well it was all right if you were five or six, but at ten-and-three-quarters you couldn't. Pulling the bedclothes up high, he closed his eyes as tightly as he could, and was amazed to find the tears still squeezing their way out. No, he mustn't. Yet he couldn't stop. The harder he tried to the more they came, and worse still, he knew he was making a noise. He stuffed the end of the sheet into his mouth and just as he thought he had stifled the sounds, his door opened and standing in the shaft of light from the landing was Anita.

'Go away,' he said.

'Can't you sleep, Johnny?'

'I said g-go away.'

'We often have homesick girls at school. I was myself when I first started, but it passes,' she said, ignoring him and coming to sit on the bed.

Johnny deliberately turned over so his back was to her, but it made no difference. Part of the sob he tried to muffle escaped.

'You needn't be afraid to cry in front of me, Johnny. I've seen lots of them cry first time away from home. It *is* your first time away, isn't it?'

When he didn't answer she said in a whisper, 'I've some chocolate in my room. I'll fetch it and we'll have a midnight feast. But keep quiet or they'll hear us downstairs.'

When she returned she was wearing a fluffy pink dressing-gown. 'Here you are.' She broke off half a bar of chocolate, 'Go on, it'll make you feel better.'

He took the chocolate and, pulling the bedclothes up to his neck, he looked at her over the top of the sheet.

'Go on, eat it. They'll send me some more when I want some.' She broke a piece from her share and popped it in her mouth. 'Fruit and nut, it's my favourite,' she said.

He ate the chocolate, still staring at the girl in the pink dressing-gown. She looked so different from the way she had downstairs when she was in a gymslip and blouse. Now her hair was flopping over the front of her shoulders and dancing about on the top button of her gown.

'How long does it take – to get used to being away?' he said.

'Depends.'

'What on?'

'I don't know what you call it, the right word, but I know what it is, how it feels.'

'You're talking rubbish.'

'I *am* not. You'll see. In a few days you' ll wonder why you ever cried at leaving home. You'll have more freedom.'

'I don't want more freedom,' he said. 'I was all right as it was.'

'Oh well.' She rose, then suddenly put her finger to her lips. 'Sshh, they're moving about downstairs. Expect they're coming to bed now. Good-night, Johnny, I'll see you in the morning.'

She leant right over and kissed him, then slid silently from the bed and went back to her own room.

Johnny put his fingers to his lips. He'd never let a girl kiss him before. Tentatively he traced the outline of his mouth, remembering the taste of her. If I have to stay here, he thought, it might not be too bad, with someone like her around. After all she hadn't turned a hair when he swore. It'll keep my bike money intact too. But I'll call her Annie, not Anita.

He slid out of bed and untied the tin hat from his case. Tomorrow he might let Annie try it on.

For the first time that day a smile raced over his face. She don't know everything, not about fresh-air holidays nor nothin', but. . . .

He laid his tin hat on the chair by the bed and patted it. P'raps we won't need it down here, he thought sleepily, if there's no bombs in the country. . . .

Winchurch, a West Country town with a population of, 4,000, had two schools, one church and three chapels, a park, library, a small museum, Victorian-built town hall, and a gracious tree-lined square where most of the shops were situated. There was one cinema and half a dozen public houses. The nearest theatre was five miles away in Bushton, but occasionally a small touring company used one of the rooms in the town hall which had a platform.

Three London schools were evacuated to Winchurch, and the following day was spent by officials, teachers and pupils from both areas, in trying to integrate the local and the evacuee children.

Mrs Dover insisted on accompanying them to school that first morning, and when she left them by the gate Anita said mischievously, 'Thought you weren't going to stay, Johnny. You said you were going back to the smoke.'

'I changed me mind. Thought I'd give it a try,' he mumbled. They walked in together. Johnny soon saw most of his mates, but Anita knew no one. All the children from one of the schools were sent to the church and chapel halls, and when they had marched away, those left were divided into age-groups. The under-nines went to one of the other schools and the over-nines stayed to share classrooms with the children in this one. When the evacuees were assessed,

Anita, who was a few months older than Johnny, went into the top class and he into the middle one.

He watched for her when school was over for the day, and left the boys he was with when she appeared, but he wouldn't go up to her. Instead he set off on the road back to the Dovers' house, for he didn't want to be seen waiting for a girl, but further along the road and out of sight of the school gates, he stopped. She caught up with him a few moments later.

'You coming back now?' he said offhandedly.

'Mmm.' Falling into step beside him she said, 'What did you think of school, Johnny?'

'OK I s'pose. Bit crowded and the locals are a dreary lot. What about you?'

'It was strange at first, but I expected it to be. Lunch-time I made a friend. Her name's Janet. She lives here in one of the houses by the park. She told me lots about the place.'

'Have they got a Saturday-morning cinema club?'

'Y-es.' Anita sounded doubtful. 'I think so, anyway. I'll find out tomorrow if you like. There's tennis-courts in the park. I'm going along with Janet next weekend, and she has a friend who owns a pony so she's going to introduce me to her.'

'Oh poo, bloody poo. Who wants to ride a stupid pony?'

Anita stopped walking suddenly and simply stood and laughed. She laughed and laughed until tears were running freely down her cheeks and Johnny didn't know what to do.

'Come off it,' he said. 'Whatever's the matter with you? Have you gone mad or something?'

'Oh, Johnny, Johnny,' she said, gasping for breath, 'I've never met anyone like you in my life before.'

Mrs Dover was watching through the window for them. 'Don't make a noise when you go to the bathroom,' she said, 'Mr Dover is working in his study.'

Anita looked at Johnny and started to laugh, but Mrs Dover had gone into the kitchen by then, and she put her hand over her mouth and ran upstairs in front of him. At the top she said, 'I thought you were going to say it again then, Johnny. You're better than the wireless, you are.'

He flung himself on to the bed in his room and wondered what they'd do now. At home he'd be out with his mates until tea-time, but here, well, he still might not stay. After all, they couldn't force him to. This evacuation lark was supposed to be voluntary, wasn't it?

It surprised him during the next few weeks just how many things there were to do. Messing about down by the stream, joining a gang of six for fights against the locals, climbing trees . . . he tended to stick with his special mates from the old school: Billy Green, Joe Ansty and Bob Tanner. Billy lived in the next street to him back home and he knew his house as well as his own. Anita mixed more with the locals, but then she didn't have any mates from school.

'Where did all the other kids from your posh school go then?' he asked her one day.

'Some went to America, some to relatives in the country, some even stayed in London.'

'Why didn't you? I mean, fancy going to a crummy old

school and being evacuated, after that posh one you was used to.'

'It wasn't posh, Johnny. Not nearly as expensive as some are. But it *was* mummy's old school and she wanted me to go there.'

'Poo, bloody poo,' he said, and watched for her to laugh. Instead she said, 'You're overdoing that phrase. It doesn't sound natural any more.'

'You nearly laughed though,' he said defiantly.

'I didn't.'

'You did, Annie.'

'Anita.'

'Anita's too bleedin' highfalutin,' he said.

'For someone who knows words like highfalutin it's a shame to spoil it by swearing.'

'I didn't bleedin' swear.'

'Yes you did. You don't even know when you're doing it, Johnny. Listen, I expect I could get you an invitation to Janet's friend's house if you like, but you'll have to behave and not swear.'

'I don't want to go *there*. I can't ride a blooming 'orse.'

'They've got a swimming-pool,' she said.

Now he *was* interested. If there was one thing he excelled at it was swimming. He went as often as he could to the baths back home, and he often thought how wonderful it would be to live by the sea and have the chance to swim every day.

'And a tennis-court, but I suppose you'll think these things too "la-di-da".' She mimicked his voice.

'Wouldn't mind having a go in the pool,' he mumbled.

'Really, Johnny? You serious?'

' 'Course I'm serious. Went swimming every day back home.'

'Did you?' She sounded surprised. 'Where?'

'In the bloo ... in the water of course, where d'you think?'

'I am a nitwit, aren't I?' she said, laughing.

As she turned away he said in a low voice, 'Well, it wasn't every day, it was about every month really, Annie, when we could afford it like. And sometimes I managed to sneak in with some others. An' I swam in the river too, whenever I could get there.'

'I think they're covering the pool over for the winter, but after, when it's warmer, I'll see if I can get you an invite,' she said.

'I shouldn't bother too much. I mean the war could be over by the summer and then I'll be back in Hackney baths and you'll be back having midnight feasts in your posh school.'

There were a lot of books in the Dovers' house and as Mr Dover was often working in his study when they came in from school, Anita and Johnny were told to keep as quiet as possible.

At first Mrs Dover didn't like them to go out to play. 'It's dark. There's the blackout. . . .' Johnny rebelled.

'It's all right for half an hour an' you'd get a bit of peace. Blimey, my mum wouldn't have wanted me under her feet all the time.'

The children won, but it was the wrong time of year for doing much, and the weekends were when they had the most freedom.

'It will be better in the summer,' Anita said to him one day, 'when the evenings are lighter. And down here we shall have the benefit of longer days.'

'How come?'

'Well, we're in Somerset, and the sun travels east to west before going down. We are the last port of call, or very nearly, Johnny. Devon and Cornwall stay lighter for even longer.'

Johnny, who had never thought about it before, was impressed. 'You're clever, you are, Annie,' he said. ' 'Course, I've never bothered to work it out like, but it stands to reason, don't it?'

When they came indoors they sat on the settee, which was almost, but not quite, as soft as that roomy armchair Johnny had sat in on the first day, and they read.

Both loved books. At home Johnny belonged to the public library and had worked his way through *Biggles*, *Just William*, and some of Charles Dickens.

'I s'pose you read Shakespeare and stuff. We did a bit at school but it don't seem real to me,' he said.

'We've done a bit of Shakespeare, too. It's wonderfully dramatic, Johnny.'

Anita brought some of her favourite books with her. 'I like the adventure books', she told Johnny, 'but I enjoy other, softer ones too. *What Katy Did* is my great favourite, and *Black Beauty*.'

The weather and the blackout combined forced them indoors early that winter, but one day when they were walking home from school together, Annie said, 'Wonder what Christmas will be like, Johnny?'

He had been pushing the thought of a Christmas away from home to the back of his mind whenever it presented itself, which was quite often lately. Now he looked at her and, realizing she was in the same boat as he was, said, 'Not too bad, I reckon. We'll be on holiday from school. Can go into Bushton, I suppose, and have a look round. It don't seem a bad town. Not like London though.'

'What did you use to do at Christmas-time, Johnny?'

He sighed deeply. 'Have a good nosh-up. Me mum makes the best Christmas puds for miles around. Then there was the mince-pies, and a chicken bursting with stuffing. Me dad always brings in a bottle or two for Christmas Day, and me and me brothers was always allowed to have a drop then. That's the only time. To tell you the truth, Annie, I don't like it much, but I never told 'em that. And we always play games in the afternoon. Me dad has a kip and when he wakes up me aunts and uncles and cousins come round and we play murder and blind-man's-buff and pork and beans. Then we have tea and pull the crackers and wear funny hats and play sitting-down games like snakes-and-ladders and things.' He paused for breath, and when she didn't speak he said, 'What do you do?'

She seemed to be gazing into space and not listening, but after a moment she said, 'Go to church on Christmas morning with Mummy and Daddy if I'm home, and in the school chapel if I'm not. We usually have a chicken and roast potatoes, sometimes we have a turkey. I don't like Christmas pudding so I just have mince-pies and cream, then afterwards we go for a walk to digest it all. We don't usually have crackers, Mummy thinks they're common, but I went out to tea once on Boxing Day and they had crackers. They were *beautiful*, Johnny, much too pretty to pull. They were red and gold and silver. I smoothed mine out afterwards and took it back to school with me next term. And they had some lovely presents inside, and paper crowns and whistles and flutes. We had a fine time that Boxing Day, but my friend moved soon after – went abroad to live.'

'That was bad luck, Annie. Must be awful having Christmas at school though. I'm wondering if I can't go home for it actually, and if I can would you like to come too? It'd be all right with me mum, I know.'

'Johnny, that is nice of you. We'd . . . better wait and see, hadn't we? I mean, we don't know yet what sort of plans have been made.'

Neither Johnny's nor Anita's parents had been to visit them yet. Billy Green's mum came one Saturday and afterwards Billy talked about when he was going home.

'But you won't go 'til the war's over, will you?' Johnny asked him.

'Might do,' he said cockily. 'We *was* talking about it. Me mum says there's not much happening and London's as safe as anywhere, she reckons.'

Johnny thought about this remark a lot. Maybe he could go back too. Then again, Billy might be exaggerating. He knew his mum was working in a factory now, that was why she hadn't yet been down to see him, and his dad was busy on the barrow all day and firewatching all night. His brothers, Jim and Ron, were both in the army, and he wished he was older and more in charge of what was to happen.

Mrs Bookman came for a visit at the beginning of December. Johnny met her at the bus station in Bushton. It was bitterly cold and the bus was late arriving. By the time it came he was starving.

'Honestly, mum, I'm ever so hungry.' he said when she opted to wait a while before eating.

'You know I'm a bad traveller, Johnny, and I couldn't face a meal yet.'

They went into a café and while she drank a cup of tea Johnny enjoyed a substantial plate of sausage and chips. There wasn't a chance for her to come out to Winchurch, 'to see me digs', Johnny said, because of the time of the return coach.

'Next time I'll come by train, Johnny,' she told him. 'That'll be after Christmas.' She gave him a carrier-bag with his presents in. 'No peeping now. Hide them until the twenty-fifth.'

Christmas wasn't as bad as he expected. The WVS laid on a huge party in the church hall, and Johnny enjoyed every minute of it. There were spam sandwiches, mince-pies and home-made lemonade. Someone dressed up as Father Christmas and handed out small gifts wrapped in pink for the girls and blue for the boys. Johnny had a puzzle like a miniature bagatelle and Anita was given a small hairbrush-and-comb set. There was even a film show – an old Charlie Chaplin film which kept breaking down.

This caused almost as much merriment to the children every time it happened as the film itself.

Afterwards Anita said, 'The crackers weren't a patch on those I was telling you about, Johnny. Didn't have such good presents in either, but they were nice. Didn't the table look gorgeous?'

Mr and Mrs Dover gave each of them a warm jumper. Johnny's was red and Annie's royal blue. Their daughter Alison and her husband arrived for Christmas dinner, and their son and his wife telephoned them after the King's speech in the afternoon. Then Alison suggested that her husband might go into the loft and find some games she was sure were still there. He emerged a quarter of an hour later with several dusty games and half a dozen equally dusty annuals. Some had belonged to Alison and some to her brother, and Anita and Johnny lay on the floor reading them when it was generally agreed to pack in playing games for a while.

Alison and her husband slept in the study. Anita helped her to set up and make two camp-beds which were kept in a cupboard there.

'I've never been in his study before' she said to Johnny when they were upstairs later that night, 'it's quite a large room, bigger than our bedrooms. He's got a gigantic desk there, with neat piles of paper and envelopes on it, and a jar filled with pencils, and guess what, they were all the same height. I specially noticed because they looked so odd. Perhaps that's why he spends so much time in there – sharpening all those pencils until they're the same size.'

Johnny thought about the pencils when he woke up

several hours later, and began to laugh quietly to himself. To his dismay the laughs became sobs and he burrowed beneath the clothes and stuffed his handkerchief into his mouth so that, in the stillness of Christmas night no one else would hear.

CHAPTER 2

1940

The snow came in January and Anita caught flu. Johnny wasn't supposed to go near her. Mrs Dover said, 'I don't want to be running up and down for both of you,' but every time he went upstairs to the bathroom he popped in to see her. He paid numerous visits to the bathroom during the few days she was confined to her bed.

'It's all gloom and doom downstairs,' he told her, 'they've just announced on the wireless that food rationing starts next week. I didn't think old man Dover *could* look more miserable, but he does.'

Anita had not been allowed comics at home, nor at her boarding-school, although she sometimes managed to see one. Her mother had told Mrs Dover, 'No comics' but Anita often bought them and hid them under the mattress. When she finished reading them, she distributed them among her friends at school. She had to be careful not to leave them around on bed-changing day, and had one or two near misses.

Johnny, who now had regular pocket money in the form of a postal order for one shilling (double what he used to get when he lived at home) and sent with his mother's weekly letter, bought *Radio Fun* for her while she was ill.

'Johnny, that's my favourite. I'll pay you.'

'No,' he said gruffly, 'it's a present. Mind she doesn't catch you with it.'

His mother didn't get down for a visit during January or February. *Working terribly hard at the factory*, she wrote, and *I can't take time off. Your dad's in munitions now too. He does-n't like working inside but hasn't any choice really, and it's all we can do to help our boys.*

'It don't seem fair us being safe down here while Mum and Dad risk being bombed, Annie.'

'That's why they wanted us to come, but what's the point if we all end up orphans?' she replied.

Johnny opened his mouth to say that she was away from her parents so much normally that it wouldn't make much difference in her case, then he had second thoughts about it.

'It's all right for you and me, we're older, but there were a lot of real tiny kids on the train, weren't there?'

'Some of them have returned, Johnny. The air-raids they expected haven't happened. *The phoney war* it said in big letters on Mr Dover's paper the other day, and I asked Miss Coventry what it meant. Quite a lot of the young children from the infants classes have gone home.'

'Mmm, I know.'

A few of Johnny's mates had gone too – Billy Green

31

among them. He went for Christmas and never returned.

Once a week the school held gasmask and air-raid-shelter drill, but so far they hadn't needed either. Sometimes they heard and saw planes overhead, but much to Johnny's disgust he never saw a dogfight and had to make do with listening or reading about them.

He discovered the date of Anita's birthday accidentally. Mrs Dover gave her a letter when they returned from school one afternoon in early March, and she pushed it into her pocket. Much later that evening when they had been sent upstairs to prepare for bed Johnny said, 'Who was your letter from, Annie?'

'From home. It looked like Mummy's writing.'

'Haven't you opened it then?'

'I forgot.'

Johnny was amazed. 'Forgot! Go on, open it now. I'm going to the bathroom anyway so you'll be nice and private, like you like.'

Anita giggled. 'Miss Coventry would be after you if you said that in her class. "Like you like indeed", she'd say, "now who can tell me the correct phrasing?" '

Johnny laughed. 'Her voice squeaks more than that. Miss Clark is much nicer anyway. As teachers go,' he added.

When he returned from the bathroom Anita had a card and a pound note in her hand.

'Tell you what we'll do, Johnny,' she said. 'We'll go to the baths in Bushton on Saturday for a swim, shall we?' She waved the note in the air.

'What's that for? Is it your birthday?'

She nodded. 'Next Monday. But Mummy and Daddy will be away then – they sent it early so I can buy something.'

'Well, you don't want to spend it on going to the baths then.' He turned to go but she put her hand on his arm.

'I do Johnny, honestly. It will be more fun to do that than to go out and buy something, really it will. And I've still got most of last week's pocket-money, so we'll have plenty.'

'No, Annie, it's yours. I got me own pocket-money.'

She shrugged her shoulders. 'OK. I'll ask Janet instead.'

'You do that.'

They were both so quiet when they came down in their pyjamas and dressing-gowns for their nightly drink that Mrs Dover asked if they were feeling well.

'You're usually chattering nineteen to the dozen,' she remarked. 'What's got into the pair of you?'

'Nothing. Just feel a bit fed-up,' Anita mumbled.

In bed that night Johnny had an idea. He would ask Mrs Dover to make Annie a birthday-cake.

She didn't slip into his room for her usual nightly chat, which was always conducted in whispers so the Dovers wouldn't hear, and when he tapped and popped his head round her door she appeared to be asleep.

'Poo, bloody poo,' he said to the picture of the Spanish lady hung on the wall opposite his bed. 'She's only a girl anyway, not me best mate.'

Nevertheless he had forgotten his chagrin the following morning, and woke early feeling very excited. It would be a surprise, this birthday-cake, and he'd buy her a present too. On Saturday, that was when he'd do it – when she went to Bushton with Janet. He would nip down to the shops in the square and have a look round.

Mrs Dover had two shocks that morning. The first was that Johnny, whom she usually had to call at least three times, was up, washed and dressed almost an hour earlier. The second was his request.

'A *birthday*-cake, Johnny?'

'Sshh, keep your voice down – I don't want her to know. I'll pay for all the stuff you use.' He waggled his head from side to side in what he hoped was a knowledgeable way. 'On Monday. Can you do it? Please?'

'It isn't money that's the problem, son. It's getting the ingredients. A lot of them are rationed – butter and sugar for a start.'

'I'd forgotten that.' He heard Annie moving around upstairs. 'OK. Leave it now and I'll work on it.'

He thought about it for most of the day, earning himself playtime detention writing out a hundred times, '*I must pay attention in class*'. It was while he was doing this, being careful to spell 'attention' as Miss Clark had at the top of the page, so as not to have to forfeit another free time, that the idea came to him. He would buy Annie a birthday-cake. He could get it from the baker in the square. They were allocated extra because it was their living – he remembered hearing that somewhere, and now he came to think about it, only last week he'd seen a big wedding-cake in the window.

He scrawled the last twelve lines and skidded down to Miss Clark's desk. 'I've finished, miss. Can I go out now?'

She looked at her watch, then smiled at him. 'Go on, you have seven minutes left,' she said.

He hugged his secret to him all the way home from school. 'I want to go into town, Mrs Dover,' he said. 'I won't be gone long.' He took the stairs two at a time, and standing on the chair in his bedroom he pulled his case from the top of the wardrobe. Frantically he counted the money in his cocoa-tin. Five shillings and sixpence. His mum had promised him some extra pocket-money when she visited, but when would that be? It was March already. Heck, he needed it now. He had already spent his two ten shilling notes on Christmas presents for his family and going halves with Annie on a plant for the Dovers.

Clattering down the stairs he heard Mrs Dover's voice (she had never become 'Auntie' to him), but didn't wait to hear what she was saying.

'Be back in half an hour,' he shouted, slamming the door and running down the path and all the way into town. He was breathless when he reached the baker's shop.

'Yes, sonny, what can I do for you?'

'I want a birthday-cake.'

'Oh, you do. Well, well. And what sort of birthday-cake had you in mind then?'

'Not too big, and I want some writing on it. I want it to say: HAPPY BIRTHDAY ANNIE.'

'Not so fast young fellow. Where do you suppose I'm going to get the ingredients for a birthday-cake from in the first place. Don't you know there's a war on?'

' 'Course I do. Aren't me two bruvvers in the army, and me mum and dad doing war-work in London; but you get extra, don't you?'

The baker leaned his elbows on the counter and rested his chin in his hands, 'Know it all, don't you? Well I can't make you a birthday-cake unless you can produce this *extra* you're on about, because I don't get it.'

'You got a cake in the window – a wedding-cake.'

The man glanced towards it. 'Quite right, sonny, so I have. I'll make you one like that if you want me to. I'll have to charge of course, and paper and cardboard are getting scarce now, but I could probably manage that! For a price,you understand.'

'Paper. You mean. . . .'

'That's right. The cake on display in the window is made from cardboard, Master Know-all.'

When he reached 14 Kerry Avenue, entering through the back door as usual, Mrs Dover was in the kitchen.

'In a tearing hurry, weren't you, Johnny? Don't you do that again. I'm responsible for you while you're under this roof, and I want to know where you are all the time. Understand?'

Anita came into the kitchen, and grinned wickedly at him. He kicked her ankle.

'Ouch.'

'Well, Johnny, I'm waiting. Where did you go?' Mrs Dover watched him.

He held back the cheeky answer that almost escaped, because he remembered in time that he might want Mrs Dover to make him a cake.

'I had to see a man about, you know, what we talked about this morning.'

'What are you on about? Now listen to me, your mother telephoned this afternoon. She's coming down to visit you on Saturday. Just as well she wasn't here today as a surprise – what she would have thought I don't know.'

'Mum? Coming here? Hey, Annie, d'you hear that? Me mum's coming in two days' time. Yippee.'

That evening after dinner Johnny helped to clear the table with Anita, as he knew was expected of him. Then he took the tea-cloth from the rail and volunteered to wipe up. If Mrs Dover was surprised she didn't show it. 'Thank you, Johnny,' she said.

Half-way through he knew he must sort the birthday-cake business out with her quickly before Annie appeared again.

'About that cake, Mrs Dover.'

'It's not possible, Johnny. But I'll tell you what I'll do. I'll make some of those cornflake cakes we had the other week. As a special treat.'

Disgustedly he clattered the cutlery into the drawer and banged the plates about as he put them away.

'Be careful Johnny, you'll break them.'

'Me mum'll make a cake,' he said. 'She'll manage it somehow.' He knew she would too, but how to get a message to her. Tomorrow was Friday – not time enough for a letter to reach her, and they hadn't a phone at home. A telegram. That was it. He could send a telegram. If he did it on his way to school tomorrow morning she'd have it within hours and she could bring the cake with her on Saturday. Then they could hide it in his bedroom until

Monday after school. He began to whistle and Mrs Dover shushed him.

'Mr Dover likes quiet while he's reading the evening paper, you know that,' she said. 'Now run along and fetch your book.'

Johnny bounded upstairs. Annie's door was ajar and she called to him as he went past.

'Can't stop,' he told her, 'I've something important to do before I come downstairs. And don't ask me to tell you about it now, 'cos I can't. It's a dead secret.'

He dragged the chair over to the wardrobe and climbed up to get his case. Annie had been scathing when she first saw it, but she had changed since then, he thought. She was OK, a real pal. It wasn't exactly her fault she'd been to a posh school before.

The cocoa tin yielded his five shillings and sixpence. A bike might have been quite good down here in the country, still he could probably earn a bit doing a newspaper-round or an errand boy's job. This was for Annie's cake and the telegram. He replaced the lid and once more clambered to the top of the wardrobe with his suitcase.

He didn't hear anyone come upstairs and go into the bathroom.

'What do you think you are doing, young man?' Mr Dover's voice almost made him fall from the chair. It wasn't often he spoke to either of them, and he certainly had not been into their rooms before.

'Getting something,' he mumbled, pushing the case well on to the top of the wardrobe and jumping down. No need for quiet now.

'Be more specific please.'

'What? I mean pardon?'

'Exactly what were you getting?'

'Something out of me case.'

'I asked you a civil question. Answer it.'

'It's private,' Johnny mumbled.

Mr Dover came closer, and Johnny moved away towards the bed. Suddenly he felt very powerful. He put one hand on his hip and faced his inquisitor. 'It's nothing to do with you,' he said.

Mr Dover pushed him on to the bed. 'You cheeky young upstart. We'll soon see about that.'

His face had turned a purple colour, and Johnny hoped he wasn't going to have a heart attack. Turning towards the door, but keeping Johnny pinioned on the bed with his podgy hand, he called, 'Ethel, Ethel, come here quickly.'

She came bounding up the stairs with Anita close behind her.

'What is it?' she asked. 'What's happened?'

'I found him hiding something on top of the wardrobe.'

'I wasn't,' Johnny said.

'What were you doing then?' She looked puzzled.

'I was getting something. I told him it's private. In my house we was allowed that. Me mum reckons everyone has their rights like.'

'Well you're in our house now, and our rules are different. What have you got in your hand?' She prised his fingers open and the money fell on to the bed; eight sixpences and six threepenny-bits.

'Where did you get that?'

'It's mine.'

'Where did it come from? You've had no pocket-money since you've been here. Not to my knowledge you haven't.'

'I *have*. It's mine I tell you. I saved it.'

'Leave him alone,' Anita broke in, 'he's already told you it's his money.'

Mrs Dover turned to her. 'How *dare* you speak to me like that. In my own house too. Oh, I knew we should never have taken evacuees, but I did think you would be all right, coming from a good school and family . . .' she looked towards her husband. 'Are you all right, William? You know you shouldn't get worked up, it's bad for your blood pressure.'

She took his arm. 'Come along, it does appear to be his own money. And you two,' she paused in the doorway and glared at them, 'as a punishment for such ill-mannered behaviour you will go to bed *now*, without your evening drink.'

Anita gathered the coins together and gave them to Johnny. She grinned at him as the Dovers left the room.

'Poo, bloody poo,' she said, and they both fell on to the bed laughing.

Mrs Dover was very cool with them the following morning, and Mr Dover was in his study with the door shut. Johnny wanted to ask what time on Saturday his mother was arriving, but thought it wiser not to risk it in case they cancelled the visit.

'I shouldn't stay if they did,' he said to Annie on their way to school.

He had his money with him, and when they reached the square he said, 'Listen, I've got to get something, something private, so you go on and I'll see you later if I don't catch up with you.'

'OK. But don't be late for school, will you?'

It was half past eight and school didn't begin until ten to nine. He hurried along to the post office but it was closed. Johnny pondered, but only for a moment; he would have to wait because once he was in class he wouldn't be able to get out on any pretext. He examined the notice by the stamp machine and discovered they didn't open until nine. It took great will power, but he didn't swear, even though no one was listening. Annie had convinced him that it was unnecessary and, well, no one could say he wasn't trying. He laughed out loud now at the memory of Annie and what she had said last night. It sounded so *funny* coming from her; but not really nice.

Concentrating his mind now on the current problem he wondered if he could sneak into the classroom without anyone seeing. No, Miss Clark always called the register early. Well, he'd say he had an important thing to do, that was the truth – and that it could only be done at nine o'clock. Miss Clark was a reasonable person – not like the Dovers, he thought, and if he told her candidly he'd probably get away without lines or anything. With luck he could be in school by ten past nine.

At ten past nine Johnny was still waiting for the post office to open. There were a lot of others waiting too, and one of them went off to telephone the postmaster to find out what was happening. At half past a little lady arrived

41

with the keys, and five minutes later she let them all in.

Although he had been there first Johnny found himself at the end of a long queue. After a while another woman came to help and things moved more quickly, but even so it was nearly ten o'clock when Johnny reached the counter.

He had written out in his school notebook what he wanted to say, but he realized it might need altering, depending on the cost. The rushed and flustered little lady who had unlocked the door helped him with it, and eventually it read: *Need cake saying Happy Birthday Annie. Please bring Sat. love Johnny.* At the last moment he cut out the word love, which he now always put on his letters to her. This reduced the message to ten words, which pleased him.

He looked at the clock in the post office when he had finished and decided it wasn't worth going to school now until dinner-time. It would take too much explaining. Maybe it would be best not to go in at all today, to pretend he had been sick. Looking around he thought what a wonderful chance it was to enjoy himself and explore a bit. He'd not had much freedom since coming here, it was only Annie who really made the place bearable. Gosh, if he had a bike. Still, he had two legs, and it was a glorious day. He set off through the square and out into the country, the real country.

Johnny had a marvellous day. The March sun was gently warm and as he swung along he whistled the way he always did back home in London. He wasn't allowed to whistle in the Dovers' house because Mr Dover always seemed to be working on someone's accounts, even though he was retired.

Johnny left his satchel behind a tree about half a mile from the town. He could collect it on the way back and be outside the school when they all came out.

Miss Clark saw Anita during the mid-morning break. 'Where is Johnny today?' she asked.

The girl looked at her in amazement. 'I – er – he wasn't too well.'

Something in Anita's attitude made her say, 'Did you bring a note?'

'Oh no, miss. He'll be all right tomorrow I expect. He – er, might even come in this afternoon. If he feels better.' she added in a rushed sort of voice.

'Thank you, Anita. Off you go then. Get some fresh air, it's a beautiful day.'

She went to the staff room where Miss Coventry was already pouring herself some tea.

'Dorothy, would you say that Anita Evesham was a truthful child?' she asked her colleague.

'Anita? Oh yes. Why?'

'Young Johnny Bookman isn't here and I simply asked her where he was today, and I'm pretty sure she was lying. But she looked so startled too, and I'm wondering now where he is and what he's up to. I mean I wouldn't put it past him to try to make his way back to London. I think he misses his folks terribly.'

'Does he? Mmm. I've not had much to do with him, of course. Anita is in my class. She is a very self-assured child for her age, and used to being away from home, I gather. The two of them do seem to be close – of course they are in the same billet. What did she tell you?'

'Said he wasn't well, but from her attitude I think she didn't know he wasn't here, and she was trying to cover for him. Maybe I'll ring Mrs Dover.'

'Can't do any harm. On the whole the evacuees have settled well, haven't they? And this term, with quite a number gone back life has been easier in the classroom.'

Miss Clark didn't have an opportunity to telephone Mrs Dover until after lunch. She had a very strong feeling that something was wrong, yet she didn't want to make a fool of herself. In the months Johnny Bookman had been in her class she had enjoyed having him there, which was more than could be said for some of her pupils. He was a lively youngster, with an unfortunate habit of swearing as part of his natural speech, but she was hoping to cure him gradually of this. Preferably before he had the rest of the class following suit. She smiled to herself as she waited for the telephone to be answered.

When it was, her fears were confirmed. Mrs Dover said he had left the house with Anita that morning at the usual time.

'What could have happened to him, Miss Clark? I know we had a bit of a to-do last night, but . . . you don't think he's run away, do you?'

'What sort of a to-do, Mrs Dover?'

'Oh nothing really. He was a bit cheeky that's all – upset Mr Dover. But he went off quite normally this morning. Have you asked Anita?'

'I will.' Miss Clark prevaricated diplomatically. 'Now don't worry and I'll do a spot of checking.'

She called into the headmaster's room on her way back to her own class, and reported. She was hesitant to do this, because she liked the lad, he wasn't bad, and she didn't want to get him into hot water with authority, but on the other hand she *was* worried about him.

The headmaster, who should have retired at Christmas but had stayed on because of the war, looked at her with a hurt expression in his eyes.

'Oh dear,' he said. 'I thought we might have problems with these evacuees. I had better see the little girl.'

Anita stuck to her story at first, then she confessed that Johnny had said he would catch her up because he had something important to do first.

'Probably a simple case of truancy,' the headmaster said to Miss Clark quietly. 'I'll have a word with the Dovers and see if he turns up after school is over. If he doesn't, then we shall need to inform the police.'

'Miss, what's happened to Johnny?' someone from the front row asked when she returned.

'Nothing, Colin, why should you think something had?'

'Well, he's not here, and he's always saying he's going back to London.'

'He'll be in on Monday,' she said. 'Now back to your books children.'

The last hour dragged. While her class were writing she had a pile of exercise books to be marked, but she found herself looking at them and seeing young Johnny's face all the time. He was an engaging little sinner, she thought. She hoped no harm had befallen him.

When the bell rang Miss Clark dismissed her class

quickly. She gathered up her bulging briefcase, locked the cupboards and desk for the weekend and hurried outside in the hope of catching Anita Evesham before she left the building. But she was too late, for Annie was already running back to Kerry Avenue as fast as she could to find out if Johnny had returned yet from whatever his important mission was.

As she ran so she prayed. 'Dear God, let him be all right,' she said. 'I couldn't bear it if anything happened to Johnny.'

CHAPTER 3

1940

'Annie, Annie, wait for me.'

Annie was travelling at such a speed she couldn't imme-diately stop. When she did, and turned round to see Johnny careering towards her, she held out her arms, but had withdrawn them by the time he reached where she was standing.

'Blimey, where's the fire,' he said.

'Johnny, where have you been?'

'Been. Why – why school, of course.'

'Oh no you haven't. Don't you dare lie to me, Johnny Bookman. Where have you been?'

'All right, Annie, but don't tell anyone. Promise? Swear on the Bible, scout's honour and all—'

'I don't need to tell anyone, they all know. A right old hue and cry there's been for you today. Don't stand there looking stupid, Johnny, we'd better get back quick, and my word you'll have some explaining to do. Why didn't you tell me you were having a day off? I could have covered for you then, properly.' She took hold of his hand. 'Come on.'

The children saw the policeman's bicycle outside number 14 as they turned the corner into Kerry Road. It was the most well-known bike in Winchurch because it was painted red, white and blue.

'Gosh, that's torn it,' Annie gasped. 'Johnny, you'd better tell the truth now.'

The constable was a local man and he knew Johnny by sight. He had made it his business to watch out for the evacuees because he thought some of the local children might gang up against them – and he hadn't overlooked the idea that it could be vice versa. He and his wife were hosts to four of them themselves, and he kept his ear close to the ground so he would know what was going on among the younger population of Winchurch.

Johnny took a deep breath, as Annie suggested, before he went in. Mrs Dover alternated between relief and anger when the children arrived.

'Thank heaven,' she said several times. 'I imagined you lying dead somewhere, and whatever would I have told your mother then?'

'Let the boy tell us where he's been,' the constable said. 'Come on son, what happened to you?'

Mr Dover had left his study when the law arrived, and was sitting by his wife's side.

'That's the trouble with the youth of today. No sense of

duty or gratitude,' he said when Johnny had finished his tale. He had omitted his reason for needing to go to the post office because Annie was in the room.

Constable Jones looked across to him. 'It did show a lack of responsibility, you know,' he said. 'You must start learning to think of the consequences before you give in to impulses like days off school. I'll let you off this time, but mind it doesn't happen again. No real harm's done, apart from wasting police time.'

'Oh, but there has been.' Mrs Dover's voice was agitated. 'I sent a telegram to his mother just before you arrived, officer.'

The policeman, who had been heading for the door, looked round. 'And what exactly did you say in the telegram, Mrs Dover?'

'Well I – I didn't say he was missing. I – I kept it short naturally because of the cost, but I did think she ought to know.'

'Be specific, Ethel,' Mr Dover's voice cut in. 'How did you word the telegram?'

'Well – I asked her to telephone me.'

Johnny breathed a deep sigh of relief. His mum would go mad if she knew what had really happened. What a mess.

'Only you can decide if you are to tell her or not,' said the policeman. 'I daresay you'll think of something to say, Mrs Dover. It's all right, I'll see myself out.'

When he had gone Johnny said nervously, 'I'm sorry for causing you all that trouble, honest. But how was I to know you'd go sending a search-party out for me?'

'That will do,' Mr Dover said. 'Go to your rooms now, both of you. Mrs Dover and I wish to talk.'

'Don't forget to change out of your school clothes,' Mrs Dover called after them.

They went upstairs and at the door to her room Annie whispered, 'Come in to me when you've changed, Johnny, and tell me all about it, won't you?'

Just as he was scrambling into his 'out of school' clothes, he heard the telephone in the hall ringing, and rushed on to the landing to listen. Annie heard it too, and they both crouched by the bathroom door, peering through the banisters straight down on to Mrs Dover's head as she answered it.

To their disappointment she kept her voice low and they heard little. Enough for them to know that it was Johnny's mother at the other end of the line, but not much else. Mostly Mrs Dover said yes and no, she certainly didn't seem to be offering any reasons for asking Mrs Bookman to telephone her earlier.

Suddenly Mrs Dover held the earpiece away from her and called up the stairs. 'Johnny, will you come here a minute, dear. Your mother would like to speak to you.'

If there had been a wide gap in the banisters Johnny would have fallen through, he was pressed so closely to them. He jumped up and rushed down the stairs, startling Mrs Dover so much that she dropped the receiver. It swung crazily at the end of the flex.

He had only used a telephone once before, and that had been with his mother's help. He picked up the dangling handset and shouted into it, 'Hullo mum.'

thought she was going to cry again while they were singing, but she didn't, although he could see the tears glinting in her eyes as she took a deep breath and blew hard.

Twice during their conversation she told him not to go away but to wait while she put more money in. And to his enormous relief she only seemed to be telephoning about his telegram, the one he had sent that morning, and she never mentioned Mrs Dover's one.

'I'll do me best about the cake, Johnny, but it won't be easy. And I can't get icing-sugar, but I'll try and fake something up for you. Exactly what do you want it to say?'

He knew Annie was listening through the banisters, and it would be a pity to spoil the surprise now, especially after all the kerfuffle it had caused.

'What I said in the telegram. Exactly that, and thanks, Mum. I knew you'd find the stuff.'

They were cut off in the middle of her next sentence, but he heard enough to know she would be in Winchurch about dinner-time tomorrow. He dashed back upstairs, where Annie was struggling into her dress.

'Yippee,' he said. 'Me mum will be down tomorrow.'

During dinner Mrs Dover asked him what his mother had wanted.

'Just to tell me she'd be here dinner-time,' he said.

'Well, you had better have your bath tonight, Johnny. And Mr Dover and I have decided, for your sake, not to say anything to her about your little escapade today. We feel sure you have learnt your lesson and the like will not happen again.'

'It is very generous of my wife to do this, Johnny, and I trust you appreciate it and will behave yourself properly in future.'

'If you hadn't panicked you'd never have known,' Johnny said. 'I'd have been home from school at the usual time and no one the wiser.'

'That is hardly the right attitude,' Mr Dover said in his measured tones. 'However, we will close the subject now, but watch your step Johnny, for I shall be watching it closely.'

Annie kicked him under the table, and he decided to take notice of her. With any luck his mum would take him back with her tomorrow, so they might as well keep things good tonight. Then there was the wonderful secret of Annie's birthday-cake. He hugged the knowledge to himself joyously.

It was late when Annie eventually crept into his room. First he had to have a bath, and while the water was hot Mrs Dover decided 'Anita must have one too.' Then she kept popping back on one pretext or another.

'I thought she'd never go,' Annie said, perching herself on the end of the bed. 'Of course she wants you to stay because she gets paid for having us and I think it's going up. Janet heard her aunt talking about it.'

'I don't care anyway. After tomorrow I shall be back home. With a bit of luck,' he added as the thought came to him that he hadn't yet mentioned this to his mother. Still, she would know that Billy and several of his old gang were back and he didn't expect trouble there.

'It won't be the same without you,' Annie said.

'They'll probably get someone else. That Mrs Poole will make them because they've got the room. Like she made them have me,' he added. 'I'm not their sort really – they

like kids what jump to it every time they speak.'

'Mmm. Wonder what sort of time their own children had, Johnny?'

'Very strict, I expect. Listen, Annie, when I go home will you write to me sometimes, let me know how you are, like?'

'If you want me to, but you haven't told me what happened to you today. Come on now, Johnny, do tell. The truth mind – why you really went off like you did. I won't breathe a word at school, honest I won't.'

'Hey, you sounded just like me then. . . .'

They were laughing about this when the door suddenly opened and Mrs Dover walked in.

'I thought so. I told Mr Dover I could hear voices. Now listen, you two. We have thrown our home open so you children can be safe, and in return we expect decent behaviour from you.'

'We weren't doing anything except talking,' Annie said.

'That's enough, miss – back to your own room, and stay there.'

Annie stood up quickly. Without looking at Johnny she walked slowly out of the room. Mrs Dover did glance once more at the figure sitting up in bed, then without another word, she too went out, closing the door behind her.

Johnny was so tired and yet he couldn't sleep. Instead he went over and over the events of the day. If only no one had questioned why he wasn't at school he would have got away with it. And the silliest part of all was that he hadn't meant to play truant, not this time. All he had wanted was

to get Annie a birthday-cake. Now he probably wouldn't even be here for her eleventh birthday. Maybe he could persuade his mum to stay over until Monday – oh heck, she'd have to go back to work by then. Johnny swore quietly to himself.

Johnny and Annie overslept on Saturday morning and breakfast was finished by the time they went downstairs.

'You can get your own,' Mrs Dover said, 'there are cornflakes and some bread and home-made jam. Don't put any marg on, it isn't necessary with jam.' Her voice sounded as if she was still cross, and her face was slightly flushed. Even her walk across the kitchen, where they always ate breakfast, towards the scullery next door, spoke of her displeasure.

'What bus are you catching to Bushton, Annie?' Johnny said when Mrs Dover was out of earshot.

'I'm not going. Not much fun on my own. Besides, your mother will be here, and if you do return to London with her, well I guess I'd just like to be around.'

Upstairs Johnny once more stood on the chair to reach his case. He packed quickly, hesitated about whether to put the rest of his money back in the cocoa-tin, and decided against it. He might be able to buy his mum a cup of tea or something on the way home. It was a long journey but he didn't mind that. It would just be so good to get back, and even if there were bombs and things, well maybe he'd dodge them. The only bleak spot in his morning was the thought of Annie. She was OK. More than OK. If he'd had a sister instead of two brothers that's who he would have

wanted. He'd never thought a lot of girls before, they were usually cry-babies who told tales and spoilt your fun. Then again he didn't know many, just some of his mates' sisters when they had to bring them along and look after them, that was all.

Back downstairs he wandered into the kitchen and looked at the clock on the wall. Time was going so slowly today. He wondered how far his mum had got. Hope she doesn't break Annie's cake, he thought, that would be awful with all the stuff on ration.

Fancy Annie's mum making her buy her own present. Not like a birthday, then. He always had a surprise, sometimes it was what he wanted and sometimes it wasn't, but he never knew until the day. He always had a birthday-cake too, and some of those iced gem biscuits he liked.

One year his brother Ron said, 'Getting too old for cakes and candles, aren't you, Johnny?'

Well, he didn't mind about the candles, but he reckoned it wouldn't seem like a birthday without a proper iced cake. He'd told Annie about it in one of their nightly chat sessions, and her eyes grew huge with wonder. So much so that he invented bigger and better cakes from other years when he was younger.

'Matron used to buy some fancy cakes if she knew it was a girl's birthday, and if she liked her,' she told him.

He couldn't wait to see her face when she had this wonderful cake with her name on.

Mrs Bookman was due at Kerry Avenue sometime during the morning. Johnny didn't know what time her

train would arrive, otherwise he would have gone to the station to meet her.

Mr Dover kept out of the way in his study, but Mrs Dover seemed to spend the morning hovering around and straightening cushions.

'Think she wants to impress your mum,' Annie said when they were alone for a few minutes.

'Whatever for?' Johnny was amazed. 'She's got a grander house than us. Not that I'd swap, ours is best any day.'

'You're very fond of your family, aren't you, Johnny?'

He looked embarrassed. 'Isn't everyone?'

'Maybe it's because you have brothers too and you're a real family.'

'Me brothers are a lot older than me, Annie. I was an accident.'

She went off into peals of laughter and he looked surprised. 'It's true,' he said, 'but once I was born it made no difference, except it kept them a bit poorer than they would have been 'cos me mum had given away all the baby things like. Do you know about having babies and all that stuff Annie?'

'I know some of it,' she said. 'The girls at my old school used to discuss it sometimes. It sounds pretty horrible.'

'Yes. Still it must be all right or people wouldn't do it.'

After all the excitement of looking forward to seeing his mother when she arrived Johnny suddenly felt irritable with himself and didn't know what to say to her. He thought she looked different too, but couldn't pinpoint

why. Unless it was her hair, he thought, as he scuffed his feet on the carpet. It was rolled into a long sausage at the back but the front bit was scraped tightly off her forehead leaving it looking as if the roots were about to spring out. He didn't like it. It didn't look like the way he remembered his mum.

They all sat in the front room until Mrs Dover rose, saying she was going to make some sandwiches for lunch.

'Come along, Anita, then you can go upstairs to your room and read a book for a while to let Johnny and his mother have some time together.'

Johnny, grateful for the chance to discuss the birthday-cake, gave everyone a big grin before shuffling himself into a more comfortable position on the sofa.

'Annie can come out with us later, can't she, mum?'

'If she wants to. I'll have to catch a fairly early train back. Don't want to be travelling across London after dark.'

'That's OK,' he said. 'I'm all packed ready.'

'Packed. But you're not coming back, Johnny. Not back to London you're not.'

'Not . . . well no, of course not. Not today, straight away like. But in a few days when it's sorted out. I – I was going to talk to you about that, but I got me things together in case you thought it was easier to come with you. When we go out I'll show you me school. But this way I'll be here for Annie's birthday on Monday so that's good.'

He leant closer to her, 'Got the cake in the bag, have you? I'll—'

'No, son, no to both. You're staying here where you are

reasonably safe, and I'm sorry about the cake but sometimes you know you ask for the craziest things.' She laid her hand on his arm in a sympathetic gesture, 'I did try, Johnny, but—'

'Ssshh,' he whispered as Annie appeared in the doorway with a plate of sandwiches in her hand.

Later both children went to the station with her. As the train pulled away Johnny felt more disconsolate even than he had when he first arrived.

'It's a shame, Johnny, but I guess she's thinking about your safety,' Annie sympathized.

He shook his head and his eyes were sad. 'No, she's not. She's enjoying the factory and she doesn't need to worry about me stuck away down here. She's got used to not having me around, I could tell. This bloody war, Annie, it's spoiling everything.'

The evening meal was ready when they returned. Johnny was quiet, but Mrs Dover made up for his lack of conversation, and Annie valiantly tried to fill in the gaps. Mr Dover, as usual simply ate, then pushed his plate away and waited for the next course.

Both children opted for an early night, and Johnny was in bed and trying not to think of the fiasco the day had been, when Annie came in.

'Do you want to talk about it, Johnny, or about something else?' she said.

'I don't know, Annie. It's been the most disappointing day of my life.'

'I'm sorry, Johnny. I know how badly you wanted to go home.' Johnny sat up in bed. He looked earnestly at Annie.

'It's not just disappointment over not going home,' he said. 'She let me down over something else that was very important.'

'I haven't trusted grown-ups for a long while, Johnny, because that's happened to me too.'

He gazed at her. 'Someone didn't do what you were absolutely certain sure they would do?'

'Well, it was more not keeping their word. When I first went to boarding-school, years ago. I didn't want to go, and I was told that if I didn't like it I could come home. I hated it, Johnny. At first I used to cry into my pillow all night. I wouldn't let anyone else see because I thought that when I wrote home and told them, they would come and fetch me.'

'And they didn't? Oh, poor Annie.'

'My mother wrote and said it was always strange at first, but that once I was used to it I would enjoy it. I tried again, but she ignored it. That's when I realized I was there for the rest of my school life, and that there never had been any intention of bringing me home if I was unhappy.'

'Here, Mum brought some chocolate down, I've been saving it to share with you.' He threw back the bedclothes and went over to the dressing-table to fetch it. 'It's only a small bar and not your favourite, but it's nice.'

'Thanks. Anyway Johnny, I wasn't looking forward to being on my own here. It will be better with the two of us.' She bit into the half-bar of chocolate Johnny gave her. 'Mmm, it's scrumptious.'

Much later, when Annie had returned to her own room,

Johnny snuggled under the blankets and allowed their conversation and confessions to wander round in his head. Compared to her life he'd had it good until now, he thought. And his mum had tried to explain about the cake – or rather the lack of it.

'It was such short notice, Johnny. I mean, if you had let me know a week before, or even three or four days, I reckon I could have done something for you, but a telegram the day before. . . .'

He fancied he could hear his own voice again. 'But on the phone you said you could.'

'I said I would try, Johnny, that I'd do me best. And I did try, but I'm working all hours now, you've got to remember that. There is a war on you know. Anyway, what's so special about this Annie?'

'Aw, nothing really. Just that it's her birthday on Monday and she ain't never had a birthday-cake of her own.'

'What you never have you never miss. Still, it was a nice idea, Johnny. Here, buy her some fancy cakes or something.' She pressed two half-crowns into his hand. 'You can get yourself something you want with the rest.'

He woke early on Sunday morning, crept downstairs and made a pot of tea for Mr and Mrs Dover. He found the tray and the biscuit-tin, took out four biscuits and carefully laid them in the saucers. Then, with a steady hand, he poured the tea.

He placed the tray on the floor outside their bedroom door. He knocked loudly, turned the handle, then quickly bent down to pick up the tray again.

He knew Mrs Dover had plenty of cooking-stuff. 'I've always kept a good larder,' he had heard her boasting to friends on the telephone not so long ago when she invited them over for a meal, 'so I'm well in hand with my rations.'

He would offer to get the breakfast too, and afterwards, maybe he'd even wash up for good measure, then he would ask her again if she would make a proper birthday-cake for Annie.

With the tray in his hands and his eyes watching the ground he entered the room, and tripped over the realistic-looking tiger-mat by the bed. With the crash of china echoing round him, and the tea and soggy biscuits soaking into the pink carpet, Johnny knew his efforts would all be in vain.

Mr Dover was cross and irritable over the incident, but his wife, to Johnny's delighted surprise, was not only reasonable, but seemed pleased.

'Not pleased that I had spilt the blooming stuff all over the bedroom carpet,' he said to Annie later, 'but that I'd bothered to make it for them.'

'Shouldn't think Mr Dover ever lifts a finger to help,' was Annie's comment.

Taking advantage of his current stock of goodwill, Johnny went through to the kitchen later in the morning when Annie was deeply engrossed in her book.

'Is there anything I can do for you?' he asked Mrs Dover.

'No, I don't think so, Johnny.'

'I was always quite useful to me mum at home.'

'I'm sure you were, son, but you know I've two chil-

dren of my own, grown-up now of course, well, you met Alison at Christmas. Anyway I learnt a few of the ways of children when they were young and I've not completely forgotten. So, tell me now what is it you want?'

'Gosh, you're OK, you are,' he said. 'Well, I'll put me cards on the table. I want Annie to have a birthday-cake tomorrow when she comes in from school.'

'Johnny, I thought we had been through all that.'

'It needn't be posh. Just a cake with her name on. And happy birthday,' he added.

'I told you I'll get some fancies.'

'You can have them anytime – well almost anytime.'

She was silent for so long Johnny thought he had lost the day, then she said, 'Would a sponge do?'

'Can it be iced?'

She sighed. 'I'll see what I can do. I'm not promising, mind. We don't get any more rations in the country than they do in the cities, except maybe eggs, which will help, but we'll see. Now off you go, and try not to antagonize Mr Dover any more today, will you, Johnny?'

He skipped out of the kitchen, then, on impulse rushed back, almost knocking Mrs Dover over.

'I just remembered. I can give you some money towards the stuff, the ingredients. If you say what they come to.'

'They won't cost too much, don't you worry about that. Now, out of the way, I've a Sunday dinner to cook, young man.'

Johnny was on his best behaviour for the rest of the day. He even did his weekend homework without being

reminded. Usually he was reading until bedtime, and had to scramble to do it before school on Monday.

'I can't understand why you don't get down to it as soon as you come in from school on Friday afternoon,' Mrs Dover often said, 'then you would know you had the whole weekend clear for any other activities. Putting off anything never does any good, it has to be done eventually. In any case you want to pass the scholarship, don't you?'

'I'm not bothered,' Johnny had said several times. 'I shall have a barrer like Dad when I leave school, anyway.'

'But you like reading and writing and talking,' Mrs Dover insisted on one occasion.

'Yes I do, but I can read when I finish work each day, and talking will be part of me job, won't it? I mean I won't have to pass the scholarship for that, will I?'

Mrs Dover smiled and shook her head at him.

On Monday morning there was no post at all for Annie. She had had her parents' card last week with the pound note, of course, but. . . .

Johnny gave her the birthday-card he had bought during the week, and that was all she had. He could hardly believe it. Why, in his house birthdays were special no matter how old you were. Birthdays and Christmas were the two highspots of the year.

The strange thing was that Annie didn't seem bothered by the lack of interest, although she did seem happy with the card he gave her. He had chosen one with a bunch of balloons on the front and had written each letter of her name in five of the balloons. Perhaps he shouldn't have

gone to all the trouble of a cake after all, he reflected, when he should have been concentrating on his English lesson. Annie was used to a different kind of life from his, and maybe what his mum had said was right, that what you didn't have you didn't miss.

They walked to school together as usual, and Johnny said as casually as he could manage, 'Have a nice day, Annie.'

'Thanks.' As she turned away to go to her classroom she said, 'Johnny, thank you for the card, it's lovely. I've got it in my satchel.'

They didn't always walk home together; often Johnny was with his pals and Annie with hers, but on Annie's eleventh birthday Johnny watched out for her. He was torn between rushing back to see if Mrs Dover had managed to bake a cake, and waiting to see if Annie was chattering to Janet. He didn't like Janet much. She treated him as though he were Annie's cross to bear – the boy who had to be looked after. But she was Annie's friend.

'She's very nice when you know her properly,' she told him, 'and she can't help her high falutin manner, as you call it. That's just the way she is, Johnny. You have to learn to take people for what they are in the end you know.'

Johnny often thought how wise Annie was. But he never let her see he thought so. He reached Kerry Avenue seven minutes before she did and almost flew in through the back door. Mrs Dover was in the kitchen.

'Goodness, Johnny, you startled me,' she said. 'Change out of your school things quickly now and then you can help me.'

By the time Annie arrived he knew there was not only a cake, but a special birthday meal. He hustled her upstairs.

'You're early Johnny,' she said. 'I looked for you on the way home.'

'I'm helping Mrs Dover, I won't be long.'

When she came downstairs fifteen minutes later Mrs Dover sent them both into the front room. 'I can manage beautifully now Johnny, thank you,' she told him.

For once Johnny's book didn't hold his attention. Usually he was so absorbed he heard and saw nothing but the characters and action of the story. Tonight, however, he was listening to every sound from the kitchen and dining-room. When Mr Dover came down from his study and put the six o'clock news on Johnny willed himself to keep absolutely quiet, for nothing must spoil this evening for Annie.

He thought she looked a bit sad, and that was under-standable. He writhed inside with excitement when he thought about the surprise she would soon have. Mrs Dover had shown him the cake when he came in from school. It was a sponge, iced in white, with HAPPY BIRTH-DAY ANITA drawn in blue. He wished she had put Annie instead of Anita on it, but still it was a cake, and it did have her name on. He hadn't bought her a present, but he intended to go into Bushton on Saturday and buy one.

When Mrs Dover came in shortly afterwards she said, 'Right, the meal's ready. Extra special one tonight because it is Anita's birthday. Come along then.'

In the dining-room the table looked magnificent. A golden-brown chicken had pride of place at one end, ready

for Mrs Dover to carve. There were three large covered dishes, a smaller open one filled with stuffing and a steaming gravy-boat. By Annie's plate was a birthday-wrapped parcel and a card. Johnny watched her.

'Oh,' she said, 'is this for me?'

'It is. Are you going to open it now before I carve?'

Annie took the paper off carefully. Inside was a white box. She lifted the lid to reveal a multicoloured necklace.

'Oh, isn't it pretty? Thank you so much.'

'I'm glad you like it,' Mrs Dover said.

'Are you going to serve that bird before it's cold?' Mr Dover's voice cut across the silence. 'She can look at her present later.'

Annie opened the card, then she smiled at Johnny. 'It's like Christmas with a chicken, isn't it?' she said.

It was a happy meal. Annie put the necklace on and Johnny thought it looked like coloured diamonds, it sparkled so when the light caught it. Even Mr Dover was moved to say, 'You had better not get near the window with it or you'll have the warden after you.'

The tureens were filled with roast potatoes, carrots and parsnips, and to everyone's surprise and delight, runner beans.

'Some I salted down in the summer,' Mrs Dover told them proudly. 'Come on now, start eating.'

When they had eaten their fill and Johnny had pronounced the meal, 'especially that stuffing' as 'scrumptious,' Mrs Dover took the plates through to the kitchen and returned with a raspberry jelly and a chocolate blancmange.

'Johnny, would you bring the rest in please?' she said, 'while I fetch the fruit bowls.'

He jumped up so smartly he almost tipped the chair over and Annie laughed delightedly. It was good to see her so relaxed and happy. He hoped she was going to like the cake, oh he did hope so.

He carried it in slowly, carefully, and with Mrs Dover's help placed it in the centre of the table. Once it was safely down he looked across to Annie and was appalled to see tears streaming down her face.

'Annie,' he said, and his voice came out as a little croak. She brushed the tears with the back of her hand.

'Isn't that wonderful,' she said, 'a birthday-cake with candles and my name on.'

Amid the laughter Mrs Dover said, 'That is Johnny's present. I was simply the cook. It was his idea.'

'I hope it tastes as good as it looks,' was Mr Dover's contribution.

'Oh it will, I'm sure it will. Can we – can we light the candles?'

'Of course.' Mrs Dover did so, and Johnny thought a table had never looked so beautiful before, the red-patterned jelly and the brown bobbly blancmange either side of THE CAKE with its eleven shimmering candles.

When they were ready to cut the cake Annie suddenly said, 'Oh it does seem a shame to touch it,' and they all laughed.

'First, Anita has to blow out her candles,' Mrs Dover said.

'And we sing Happy Birthday,' Johnny added. He

CHAPTER 4

1941

Johnny stepped from the train at Winchurch station and dived down the slope at the side.

'Hey, where d'you think you're going? Oh it's you, Johnny me lad. Well the exit is over here.' Old Mr West caught up with him and ruffled Johnny's hair.

'I know, Mr West, but it's quicker this way. Anyhow, I got me ticket. I'm not getting a free ride.'

'Where you been?'

'London. Back home to me brother's wedding.'

'Oh yes. You were best man, I suppose?'

'No I wasn't. Me other brother was though. He got special leave. It was a smashing do.'

'Go on, off you go, and mind you go straight there.'

Johnny hurried down the slope and set off for Kerry Avenue. It had been wonderful to be home again, and he'd got some even more marvellous news to tell Annie. But he'd pick his time, and it wouldn't be when the Dovers were listening.

They all seemed pleased to see him. Strange, that, he thought. Even Mr Dover talked a bit over the meal. Johnny winked at Annie, and she grinned back at him. They both knew they would catch up with each other's news when they went upstairs to bed that night, but Johnny's excitement was such that he couldn't wait that long. He passed a note to Annie saying, 'Something to tell you, can you escape?'

After a while she left the room saying, 'Will you excuse me for ten minutes, please? I have some work in my satchel to sort out.'

When Johnny rose a few minutes afterwards, Mrs Dover asked where he was going.

'To unpack my case.' He was careful to say 'my' and not 'me' and he kept his face sober and his voice quietly pitched.

'Gosh', he said, when he and Annie were alone, 'it seems as if I've been away for longer than a weekend.'

'It went off all right then?' she said.

'Oh yeah, smashing. And I've got a sister-in-law now. She's a bit of all right too. Jim can certainly pick 'em.'

Annie turned away.

'What's up?' he said.

'Oh nothing.'

'Yes there is. I can tell.'

'All right then. It's the way you said that. As though your brother picked a wife like – like buying a pound of potatoes. I expect they got married because he loves her.'

'Well 'course 'e does, silly. But she's a looker too. You should have heard what me other brother was saying about her. He got a thirty-six-hour pass to be best man, but Jim got a week 'cos he was the groom.'

'You enjoyed it all then? The wedding and being home?'

'Yep. Mind, I nearly didn't bother to come back to this dump.'

'Why did you, then?'

Johnny shrugged. 'You really want to know?'

Annie nodded, watching him.

'Well it was you. I didn't want to never see you again.'

He swung his case on to the bed and started whistling 'Run, Rabbit Run', as he undid it and scattered the contents about. Annie sat on the edge of the bed and watched him.

'I'm glad you did come back, Johnny,' she said after a few minutes.

'Here.' He took a bulky-looking shape wrapped in a teacloth from his case. 'I got you something.'

She undid it carefully. Inside was a piece of wedding-cake, a silver shoe and some rose-petals.

'That's what they used for confetti,' Johnny said offhandedly, 'real rose-petals. Thought you'd like a bit of the wedding seeing as how you missed all the excitement. And it was a proper wedding-cake. My mum and Doris's mum got together and saved all their coupons for months to get the stuff.'

'Gosh, thanks Johnny. I kept wishing I could come with you. It seemed a long weekend with only the Dovers for company. They're ever so dull.'

'That's the other exciting news, Annie. Me mum says

you can come for the weekend when I have me birthday treat next month. We're going to a show and we'll probably eat out too, seeing as how it's a special occasion.'

'Come up and stay with you?'

Johnny sauntered as nonchalantly as he could over to the door.

'Of course. It'd be too late to come back here after the theatre. Mind, there's danger in London, the bombs falling, you'll probably want to think about it first.'

'Oh no, Johnny, I don't need to think about it. I'd love to come.'

He turned to face her so suddenly he almost fell over himself. 'Smashing.' he said. 'We'll have a whale of a weekend. You can help me choose what we go to see, and we'll have a slap-up meal.'

'Sshh Johnny, keep your voice down or you'll have sir and madam up to "see what is going on".' Annie gave a fair imitation of Mrs Dover's voice. They went downstairs again, and for the rest of the evening they gave each other excited glances.

Later, at their nightly chat session Johnny told her how excited his mum had been to have all the family home together, even though it was only for the weekend.

'And the siren didn't go once during the wedding, but it did in the night, though there were no bombs dropped near us. Just heard the planes going over, that's all. Didn't see any action.'

Johnny's twelfth birthday was actually on the Wednesday, but the jollifications were arranged for the weekend when Mrs Bookman would be home from the factory where she worked.

Annie's parents were hesitant when she asked permission to spend the weekend in London with the Bookmans. Mrs Evesham had a long telephone conversation with Mrs Dover one evening and at the end of it Mrs Dover said, 'Anita, your mother would like to speak to you.'

Johnny went upstairs, ostensibly to go to the bathroom, but in reality to squat on the landing and peer through the banisters. Looking down on to the mass of Annie's shining dark hair he thought, I bet they'll stop her coming with me, yet her mum never comes to see her and only writes once a month. She doesn't really care about her, not like I do.

This discovery made him feel strange from head to toe. He even shivered a little. Yes, he did care about her, in fact he couldn't imagine life without Annie now. She was better than his own mates because not only did she join in with any adventure that was on the go, but he could talk to her as well. And looking at her, as he was now from his vantage point, a heady, vibrant sensation shot through him and he felt the blood suffusing his cheeks at the temerity of his thoughts. *Annie Evesham, I believe I'm in love with you.*

He waited until he heard her say, 'Goodbye, Mummy,' and disappear into the front room before he came downstairs. She looked across to him as he entered and, smiling happily, she said, 'I can come, Johnny.'

It was hard not to rush over and swing her round and round as he had in that dancing sequence at school last week, but instead he simply said, 'That's good.'

She took him to task about this when they were upstairs again later.

73

'You didn't show much enthusiasm when I said I was allowed to come and spend the weekend at your house, Johnny. I thought you wanted me to.'

He laughed delightedly, feeling power too now for the first time in his life. 'I do, Annie,' he said, 'you know darn well I do, but it's best not to let the others see that. If grown-ups think you want something very badly they'll try to stop it, pretending it's for your own good.'

Mrs Dover made a great deal of the proposed weekend in London. 'I'm sure I think you're very brave, the both of you,' she said several times. 'You wouldn't catch me going up there unless it was necessary. Certainly not to go to the theatre.'

'And have dinner in a restaurant,' Johnny said proudly. 'No messing about with rations and things. I shall eat enough to last me for days.'

Annie laughed delightedly. 'If you're too greedy you'll be sick and then it won't have been any pleasure at all.'

'My stomach's strong. You'd be surprised at what I can put away,' he boasted.

'You are both forgetting that it costs money to eat out,' Mrs Dover said.

'It's me birthday treat. I'm having a theatre visit and a meal out instead of a present.' Johnny looked smugly at her. 'Me mum's earning a lot of money in the factory now and we've never been terribly poor like some kids are. We've always had enough to eat and decent clothes.'

In the two years Johnny had lived with the Dovers he had grown much taller and lost some of what Annie called his 'sloppy speech habits'. His natural accent was still there, and he spoke as quickly, but he didn't swear as much and Annie had shown him the beauty of words.

Although she was used to bucking authority, she had never done it with such joy until she met Johnny. Until then it had been a grim 'I won't let you beat me' attitude. Now it was happy, shared excitement.

Together they had taken several afternoons off school and gone to the pictures. Annie always had money sent to her by her parents. They spaced these visits out and had only been caught once. 'And then we didn't let on where we'd been,' they enthused to each other later, for Annie had quickly said that she had hurt her foot and Johnny had stayed with her until she could walk on it again.

'Mind, I don't think they believed us,' she said later, 'but who cares. They couldn't prove I wasn't speaking the truth.'

'You're better at that than I am,' he had answered then. 'Me mum always says she knows when I'm telling a lie.'

'So do I,' she answered solemnly.

'How? Come on – give.'

'Ouch, let go, you're hurting my arm.'

Johnny stopped immediately. He couldn't bear to hurt her. He had never felt like this about a girl before. Not about anyone really. 'Tell me how you know, Annie. An' – and I'll tell you if you're right,' he finished triumphantly. 'That's fair.'

'I suppose so.' She put her head slightly to one side, a habit he had noticed before when she needed time to think. 'Well, you lapse into cockney, but . . . it's hard to say really – more than usual. Sort of emphasized.'

' 'Course I don't,' he answered loudly. 'You just think I do. Why, I even sound my h's properly now. It's your imagination. You ought ter write stories, cor struth you did, Annie. You wouldn't 'alf be good at it.'

They were to leave for London early on Saturday morning and return to Winchurch on Sunday afternoon. Annie had by now met Mrs Bookman several times, when she had come down to Winchurch on her day off to see Johnny. She liked her.

'She startled me at first she was so quick,' she confided to Johnny, 'but she's definite, goes straight to the point and when she laughs I could laugh too without even knowing the joke.'

Mrs Dover tried to persuade Johnny to borrow one of their suitcases, but he refused to be parted from his well-worn one.

'I don't know why. This is smarter and will hold more,' she said.

'Mine holds enough, thank you, Mrs Dover, and I like it.'

'Hey, are you going to take your tin hat, Johnny? You might need it in London,' Annie said when they were packing. He grabbed the nearest pillow and threw it at her.

They left the house on Saturday morning with Mrs Dover's voice following them down the garden path. 'Be careful on the roads up there.'

'That's rich, that is,' Johnny said when they had turned the corner, 'worrying about the London traffic when there's bombs blowing up all around you.'

'Johnny, you do exaggerate. Come on, let's run, I can't wait to get there.'

On the station waiting for the London train she said suddenly, 'Does this sound absolutely awful to you? I'm hoping there will be a raid while we're there. Just a little one, not people getting killed or injured, but German planes coming over and our guns shooting at them. Think how exciting it would be, Johnny?'

Johnny, whose thoughts about the weekend at home had not been along those lines felt amazed for a few moments. Fancy wanting to go into danger like that just for the hell of it. Annie was quite a girl.

Mrs Bookman was at Paddington station to meet them. She threw an arm round each very quickly, then releasing them, she clenched her fist and shadow-boxed her son's chin. That nearly made him cry, and he wanted very badly to tell her he missed her too. Instead he said loudly, 'Hey Mum. Annie's hoping there'll be an air-raid while we're here.'

Annie looked embarrassed. 'You make it sound wicked, Johnny, and I didn't mean it like that.'

Mrs Bookman turned to here. 'There probably will be,' she said, 'but I think I know what you mean, duck – not much excitement stuck down there in the country. I'd hate it meself.'

They travelled by tube and bus back to Johnny's home in Hackney.

'D'you want to see your mum while you're up here, Annie?' Mrs Bookman said as the tube raced through the blackness.

'No, thank you. They're away at present. I spoke to her on the telephone last week, though.'

Once indoors Johnny thought how small everything looked. The two-up, two-down terraced house had always seemed roomy to him before. Bigger than the homes of some of his mates, who lived in the flats anyway.

Now it felt very poky. Still, it was good to be back. To hear his mum singing away to the wireless and to see again his home-made ships and racing-cars. Before the war he had shared a bedroom with his two brothers. Now they were both in the army he'd have it to himself.

'I've put Annie in the bedroom, Johnny,' Mrs Bookman said now, 'and you'll be in the bedchair down here tonight.'

Oh well, you couldn't win 'em all and he hadn't really thought about where Annie would sleep. Just to be home was good enough, and he'd slept on the bedchair often before; it wasn't too hard, unless you turned over suddenly and caught your face on the arm.

'When we going up West then Mum?'

'When we've had something to eat. I've got some dried egg so I thought I'd do you scrambled egg and chips now and we'll have tea out before we go to the show.'

'I am looking forward to it, Mrs Bookman,' Annie said quietly, 'and it is good of you to invite me too.'

'It's a pleasure, Annie. I just hope those blighters stay away tonight, that's all. It's been much better lately. It's such a relief to know you kids are safe down there in the country. I expect your mum feels the same.' Annie didn't answer.

They both helped to wash and wipe up, then they set off for the West End. They had seats booked for *Applesauce* at the Palladium. 'Second house,' Mrs Bookman told them, 'because I wasn't sure if we'd make the first at half past two. But this starts at twenty past six so it'll give us time for a meal first. I know a nice little place where we can eat. It's small but the food's good. Unless you want to go to Lyons Corner House. They have a band there.'

The subject of where to eat lasted almost until they were in Oxford Street, the smaller place eventually winning when Mrs Bookman told them about the chocolate éclairs with real cream.

'I've only been there once meself, but it was good,' she said, 'and it's handy for the theatre. Don't want too far to go, do we?'

They had a wonderful afternoon. 'It's smashing to be in London again,' Johnny said, 'though to be fair the country's not bad. More to do than I'd thought there'd be. Which do you like best, Annie, forgetting about being away from home I mean. Just supposing you could have a choice like, after the war?'

'The country, Johnny. It's quieter, not so smoky, and you can keep animals.'

'You like animals, Annie? What, sheep and things? Because you can keep cats and dogs in town, can't you?' Johnny's mum smiled across at her.

'Yes, but with me it's horses mostly, Mrs Bookman.'

'Call me Mum, or Mrs B or something,' she said. 'Mrs Bookman's such a mouthful. Horses, eh – I like horses too. Have you got one at your home?'

'No. But I can ride. I used to have lessons, and there's a girl at school sometimes lets me ride her pony.'

'I wouldn't have minded doing that. Oh, I can't ride, but I'd have loved to try. Still, it's a different world in the country and maybe I wouldn't enjoy it for long. You go where the Lord puts you, don't you?'

Johnny thought his heart would burst. He wasn't sure whether with excitement or happiness, just to be back walking the streets of home. To make a perfect day it needed his dad and brothers there too, but Jim and Ron were both overseas now, and, like his mum often said, 'You can't have everything.' He would see his dad tonight anyway, and tomorrow morning, because he didn't work on Sundays. Anyway, if they were all there he'd probably be in trouble for something or another, he thought, he usually was.

'How's Doris, Mum?' he said, and, turning to Annie, 'That's me sister-in-law.'

'I know. You never stop telling me.'

'She's OK, Johnny. Working in the factory with me in the week, and usually goes to her mum's at weekends. And I heard from Ron *and* Jim the other day. Not much, but they're both all right. Thank God you're not old enough yet to go in the forces.'

She turned towards Annie. 'Jim and Ron, our other sons, are both overseas now,' she said to her.

They gave themselves plenty of time before the theatre for their tea.

'Oh, it's lovely, isn't it?' Annie said when they were inside the little restaurant with its red-plush wallpaper and white tablecloths. The waiter was elderly with a thatch of white hair and a charming manner. Both children studied the menu for so long that Mrs Bookman suggested she should order for them.

'No mum – I know what I want but it's nice to see what else you could have. If you weren't having what you are having, I mean.'

Mrs Bookman and Annie went into a fit of giggles at this piece of logic and it was a very jolly party who eventually tucked into steak-and-kidney pie, potatoes and vegetables.

'Leave enough room for your éclair Johnny.' Annie laughed as he wiped the last piece of pie on his fork round the plate.

The éclairs, when they arrived, looked every bit as scrumptious as Mrs Bookman's description of them. Johnny looked at the silver cake-fork by his plate, then watched to see what Annie would do.

'Mmm, this looks gorgeous,' she said. She picked up the fork and cut into the éclair's creamy centre just as the air raid warning sounded. Johnny and Annie looked at each other then turned to Mrs Bookman who was already pushing back her chair. The waiter clapped his hands for attention.

'We have a deep cellar,' he said loudly, 'anyone who wishes to use it please follow me.'

Some customers stayed at their tables but Mrs Bookman ushered the children to join others who were following the waiter through to the back of the premises. Not sure whether to take the cake with him Johnny saw no one else had done so, and with a mouth-watering glance at the gleaming richness of the chocolate éclair on his plate, he tagged along behind Annie.

They reached the kitchen doorway just as an almighty noise rumbled around and the ceiling caved in on them.

CHAPTER 5

1941

'Johnny, Johnny where are you?'

'Annie, I'm here but I can't see you. Where's me mum?'

Both children called for her, but the only sound was of someone moaning.

'Mum, are you OK?' Johnny began crawling towards the sound.

A man's voice answered. 'It's my leg – I can't move my leg.'

'Wait,' Johnny said. 'Someone'll be here in a minute. It must 'ave bin a bleedin' bomb. Annie, Mum, answer me for God's sake.'

His eyes were gradually becoming accustomed to the gloom and when he crawled on to something soft Annie's voice, very close, said, 'Johnny, is that you? Can you lift this thing off me, it's squashing my arm.'

He fumbled around, trying to feel the shape of whatever

was pinioning her. 'Are you hurt Annie?'

'I – I don't think so. Are you? And – and what about your mum?'

A beam of light suddenly flashed on to the children and a deep voice said, 'Over here, Bert.' Then softly, 'Don't worry, we'll have you out into daylight in a jiffy.' The light from the torch swung round on to Johnny, on his hands and knees in the rubble that had been the restaurant.

'You all right, son?'

'Yes, but I can't find me mum.'

'Stay still while we get the little girl out, then we'll look.'

Another warden joined him, and together they lifted the beam that had trapped her. Five minutes later both children were in an ambulance *en route* for the hospital, Johnny protesting that he couldn't go without his mother.

'Tell me your name, son, and we'll see you meet up, but we've got to get this ambulance away now. And don't worry, we'll tell her you're both all right and where they've taken you.'

The ambulance doors closed and Johnny and Annie, together with half a dozen others, all of them covered in dust and plaster, were on their way.

At the hospital they set Annie's broken arm, checked the cuts and grazes on them both, then told them to wait. A WVS lady came along within minutes and gave them a drink of cocoa each.

Johnny turned to Annie. 'How d'you feel, Annie?'

'I'm – I'm not sure, Johnny. All right, I think. It doesn't hurt now.' She glanced down at her arm, encased from the wrist to just above the elbow in plaster.

'D'you feel like coming with me to look for Mum? I'm bloody worried about her.'

'D'you suppose . . .' her eyes were dark with fright.

'I don't know, do I? And now they've fixed you up they aren't going to bother – there's people in worse states than us. But I've got to find her.'

Annie was hesitant. 'We ought to stay and let them find her, Johnny. It will disrupt things otherwise.'

'You stay, then, I'm going to look for her.'

'Johnny, wait for me, I'm coming with you.'

In the waiting-room of the hospital where the staff had left the walking casualties of the bomb, several people watched the children go. Most of them looked dazed, and if they thought they ought to stop them none was yet thinking well enough to do so. The WVS ladies had moved on and Johnny and Annie walked quietly out.

Johnny's main thought was to get away from the hospital and back to the restaurant, where he was sure his mother was still somewhere in the building. Perhaps the wardens had dug her out by now, if so she would be going frantic looking for them, and if they hadn't, then he must return to find her. Beyond that his mind refused to think.

'I wonder where we are?' he said to Annie. 'I don't suppose they brought us far, do you?'

'The – the restaurant was – was just off Oxford Street, Johnny. Maybe we should ask someone.'

It was dark now and Johnny stopped the first person he heard and dimly saw coming along.

'Oxford Street. Turn right at the next corner and keep

straight on. It's a long road though. Which part do you want?'

'Near the Palladium.'

'I should catch a bus, son. Any one along here will take you. Does your mother know you're out?'

'Oh yes,' Johnny answered quickly. 'We're going to meet her now.'

They had been walking for about five minutes when Annie said, 'Johnny, I feel bad. I think I'm going to faint.'

'Oh Gawd. Annie, you mustn't. Look we're nearly there. Hang on to me.'

'Let me stand still for a minute. I'm so cold.'

Johnny was frightened. Suppose Annie died on him. Whatever was he going to do. Well, for one thing he was going to find his mother. Perhaps he should have left Annie at the hospital. Maybe she was injured worse than he knew.

'Annie. D'you feel better, gal?'

'Yes. I'm all right now, but don't walk so quickly, Johnny. I expect it's the shock. I've never fainted, but I came over so queer then, I thought perhaps that was what was happening to me.'

'Hullo then, and where are you two off to?'

The large policeman who loomed out of the darkness and shone his muffled torch in their startled faces reached out a friendly arm. Johnny, who now felt that every adult was out to stop him reaching his mother, took Annie's good hand and, pulling her with him, ran down the first turning he came to.

He turned off from this and, still half dragging, half

supporting Annie off from the next one too. A few minutes and a few turnings later Johnny pulled Annie into a shop doorway. 'I think we've lost him', he said. 'Are you OK, Annie?'

'Yes, Johnny. But why did you run from the policeman. He could probably have taken us to your mum. Now we might never find her.' To his great consternation Annie, calm matter-of-fact, cope-with-anything Annie, burst into tears.

'Annie, please don't cry. Please. Please.' He had his arm round her and she was still shivering. 'Look, we'll find somewhere you can sit and rest – a café or something, and I'll go and look for Mum.'

'Oh Johnny, do you suppose I b-brought that air-raid on by what I said this morning?'

'W-what d'you mean? What did you say?'

Annie swallowed her sob. 'You know, when I said, I'd like to experience one.'

'Of course not,' he said softly into her ear. 'You don't 'alf talk some bloody nonsense sometimes, Annie.'

'Johnny, don't leave me here. I don't suppose there's a café open anyway. I'd rather come with you. I'm all right now, honest.'

He could feel her still trembling beneath his hold. 'All right,' he said, 'but we've got to get out of this area soon or that copper will find us and we'll be back with them all trying to hush us up. See – if me mum's . . .' he swallowed hard, took a huge breath and said quickly, 'if she's dead then I want to know. Come on.'

Silently and cautiously the children left the doorway

and started walking again. This time, although they passed a few people, they did not ask the way. After they had been going for some twenty minutes Annie said, 'Have you any idea where we are, Johnny?'

'No. But we can't . . .' The wail of the siren interrupted him and they both stopped immediately.

'Must be another raid,' Annie said, 'I never heard the All Clear for the last one. And Johnny, I'm all right. Look I'm not shaking any more. Stupid to be so silly.'

He couldn't actually see her face but he looked in that direction. ' 'Course you are,' he said, 'I knew you would be. You're a great girl Annie. You're my girl, aren't you?'

She didn't answer for a moment and he said, 'Come on, we'd better keep going.'

She looked skywards. 'There's no sign of any activity Johnny.' As she spoke searchlights swept across the heavens and they felt for each other's hands.

'They have street shelters up here,' Johnny said, his voice a little catchy, 'me mum told me. We'll dive into one of those if we see a Jerry. 'Til the all clear goes, like.' His voice grew stronger, 'Don't suppose anyone'd take any notice of us there because all sorts who were caught out would go.'

They were now in a street with many small shops, and when, suddenly they heard the planes overhead they held on to each other's hands and sheltered in one of the doorways. As Johnny held Annie tightly to him she whispered, 'What you said Johnny, about me being your girl. Well, just in case they get us this time I want you to know that I am. I want to be your girl.'

Overhead the sound of aircraft continued, and the children huddled together in the shop doorway, waiting for the bombs to fall. When nothing happened and the sound of the engines had died away they were amazed.

'I thought that was our lot, Annie.'

'Me too. But they've gone over.'

'W-what do we do now? How's your arm?'

'Not too bad. It doesn't really hurt now. I suppose the plaster is supporting it.'

'Annie.'

'Yes.'

'D'you suppose Mum's dead?'

'I hope not. Oh, I hope not.'

'She wasn't in that lot they brought to the hospital. We were there quite a long time and I watched everyone who came in while you were having your injuries seen to.'

'They might have taken her to another hospital, Johnny.'

'No,' he said, 'she'd have come in to where we were – and she didn't.'

'Look, Johnny, we'd best find someone to help us, or else go back to your house. I've got some money – oh, my bag, Johnny, it's gone! I've lost my handbag and it's got my money and our return tickets in it.'

He put his hand in his trouser-pocket and jingled some coins. 'I've got some, Annie. Don't worry. But I don't know what time it is or – or anything.'

He was very close to tears too now, fighting hard to keep them back. 'Let's wait here 'til the All Clear goes,' he said, 'then we'll try and find a bus-stop. If we get back on that main road where we were before it'll be easy as pie.'

They sat down on the tiles in the shop doorway, and Johnny put his arm round Annie. 'All right?' he asked her.

'Yes. Are you?'

'I am now. You try to sleep for a while and I'll keep watch.'

Five minutes afterwards they were both asleep.

The policeman found them there an hour later. It wasn't the one who had chased them, but he was nevertheless looking for two children who had walked out of the hospital when they were left unattended. Gently he tapped Johnny on the shoulder. 'Come along, laddie, I'll take you home. What's your name?'

He was a large policeman, tall, fat, authoritarian, and he was straddled across the doorway, blocking the children's way out. Johnny was tired in spite of his snooze and this time he gave in easily.

'Johnny Bookman, and this is Annie Evesham.'

'I thought it might be. Well, come along and we'll find you something to eat and drink at the station while we're waiting for your mother.'

Annie was struggling to her feet by this time, and Johnny said, 'She was with us in the restaurant when the bomb fell.'

'So I gather. And she's been looking for you two ever since.' He held on to Annie's good arm on one side, and one of Johnny's on the other.

'You – you mean, she's alive?'

'Yes, son. And worried sick about the pair of you, I gather. She expected to find you in the hospital, see. A right old turn-out this is.'

He took them to a police station a few minutes' walk away and telephoned from there to the hospital to say they were safe.

It was late by the time Mrs Bookman collected them. They were drinking cocoa and exchanging riddles with the desk-sergeant when she came in. She threw her arms round Johnny and hugged him so tightly it actually hurt, then quickly she turned to Annie and engulfed her too. 'You bloody fools,' she said through her tears, 'you should have waited at the hospital.'

CHAPTER 6

1941

Back at school on Monday Annie came in for a lot of attention.

'What have you done to your arm? How did you do it?' Both children became the centre of interest when they told of their adventure to an admiring audience in the playground.

'Were you injured too, Johnny?' someone asked.

'Just a few bruises and scratches really,' he said, in what he hoped sounded a 'making light of it' voice.

'Gosh. A good job you'd eaten your meal before the bomb fell.'

'Annie was just biting into her éclair and Mum and me hadn't started ours. What a waste,' he said. 'You should have seen the size of them. Huge, weren't they, Annie?'

'And we didn't get to see the show either,' Annie joined in. 'But I guess we were all lucky not to be killed.'

'Was it a direct hit, Anita?'

'No. Wouldn't have stood much chance then. The bomb fell further along the road, Johnny's mum said afterwards. She wasn't injured, well a few bruises and cuts, because she was sort of thrown around away from where we were and we got separated. They took us two in one ambulance and Mrs Bookman in another.'

'And she was in a different part of the hospital from us,' Johnny added, 'but we didn't know this at the time. We thought she was still at the restaurant – buried underneath the debris,' he finished dramatically, 'so we went back to search for her.'

'Gosh.'

'Did you really? Weren't you afraid?'

The bell broke up the playground session, and Annie and Johnny returned to their respective classrooms, glorying in their brief moments of celebrity prestige.

The Dovers were also impressed and made a great deal of fuss of both children. Mrs Dover especially, who later in the week suggested she should take them to Bushton on Saturday.

'We might be able to lose her for a while,' Annie said later. 'We must make a plan. Tell you what, on Saturday you follow exactly what I say and do and just go along with it. OK, Johnny?'

'OK. We don't want her tagging along. We could just as easily go in on our own anyway.'

'But she wants to give us a treat, Johnny. It's a kind thought and, well, I expect we can manage to dodge spending *all* the time with her. Have to do what she wants for some of it, I expect. Leave it with me and I'll work something out.'

Johnny was content to do this. He realized that Annie had the kind of brain that coped with this sort of thing. She sorted out the details whereas he took a chance, and often it backfired on him, like the morning of the post office fiasco.

They went in on the ten o'clock bus on Saturday morning, and Annie whispered to Johnny to be patient for the first half-hour and she was sure they could then get away on their own. After a sedate walk along by the river Annie suggested to Mrs Dover that she might enjoy a cup of tea in the small café there. 'I should like to treat you to that,' she said, smiling at her foster-mum, and secure in the knowledge that, in spite of losing her purse in the bombing, today her pocket-money had arrived and before she left Mrs Bookman had given both her and Johnny half a crown each. She had not taken all her money to London with her in any case, and she looked appealingly at Mrs Dover (she had never been able to bring herself to call her 'auntie' either) and added, 'It won't be much fun for you to have to be with us all the time. I expect you'd like half an hour's break and we'll be fine just having a look round.'

'Well I suppose you can,' Mrs Dover said when they were in the café, 'but be careful of the roads now, and be sure and be back here by—'

'By lunch-time,' Annie interrupted swiftly. 'That will give you a chance to do any shopping and have a rest, won't it?'

They had brought sandwiches with them which were

going to be eaten by the river. 'I promise we won't be late. We'll be here by half past one.'

'By one o clock, Anita,' Mrs Dover said firmly, 'and don't get up to any mischief, mind.'

They left her drinking her tea and, once outside, skipped joyfully across the grass and down to the riverbank.

'What shall we do now?' Annie said. 'We've two whole hours.'

'Let's have a boat out. I'll row and you can sit and do nothing but nurse your plastered arm.'

Annie giggled. 'It would be fun. Tell you what, let's have a look round the town first. There's lots of nice shops and an amusement arcade, and if we have a boat now Mrs Dover might see us when she leaves the café.'

'Good thinking, gal,' Johnny was in one of his showing-off moods. 'I can get me mum a card – a nice picture of the river. Poor old Mum, she was as worried about us as we were about her last week.'

'Yes, we mucked that up properly between us, didn't we, Johnny? It's all right now, thinking about it, but it was very scary at the time.'

They went into the amusement arcade and Annie changed two shillings into pennies and halfpennies. She gave Johnny a shilling's worth. 'Here you are. When we've spent this we'll do something else, shall we?'

'I've got some of me own,' he said.

'Go on, I've changed it into coppers now.'

They had a go on almost everything and when they won and a shower of money tipped into the chute they gathered it gleefully, divided it and spent it again.

Eventually they emerged into the High Street and wandered along looking in the shop-windows. Annie pressed her nose closely against one which held a fascinating array of objects; jewellery, toys, ornaments, flimsy georgette scarves, paintings, crystal balls. . . .

They went inside and although it was quite small it was an Aladdin's cave of treasure. Annie seemed drawn to the jewellery. She tried on a bracelet, a ring, fingered a snaky necklace, and when Johnny joined her he picked up the ring, a silver band with a deep ruby-coloured stone set in it. 'That's lovely,' he said.

'Yes, it is.' She held out her hand for him to give it to her, but instead he awkwardly took hold of her fingers and tried to put the ring on. She giggled nervously. 'It's the wrong finger, Johnny, it won't fit that one. This one's thinner.' Together they put it on the third finger of her left hand.

Johnny swallowed loudly. 'D'you like that ring, Annie?'

'Mmm. It's pretty, isn't it? It looks right.'

He let her hand go abruptly and fished about in his pocket for his money. 'I'll buy it for you,' he said. 'How much is it?'

The shopkeeper, a wizened little old man had been watching them discreetly. Now he moved forward and Johnny said, 'How much is this ring, please?'

'Half a crown.'

'Right. We'll take it.' Johnny handed over the money, and they walked out and into the bright sunshine of the High Street again.

'Gosh, thanks Johnny.' Annie looked down at the ring

gleaming now on her finger. 'It's beautiful.'

'It means you're my girl, Annie. No messing about with other boys now.'

'I won't, Johnny. I like being your girl.'

They returned to the riverside and asked the man in the boat-hut how much it cost to hire a rowing boat for half an hour.

'Can you row?'

'Yes,' Johnny replied.

'Not safe for her to go out with an arm in plaster. No.'

'But I'll be rowing the boat—'

'I said no. Now be off with you.'

Disconsolately they turned away and Johnny muttered, 'Silly old bugger. He's no right to stop us. We can swim and anyway I'm not going to turn the bloody boat over.'

'Johnny, why do you always swear when you're cross or excited or upset? I wish you didn't – it sounds horrible.'

'Poo bloody poo.'

In spite of herself Annie started to laugh, and within minutes they were both doubled up with laughter.

Johnny recovered first. 'You're so funny when you're acting posh Annie. It's natural to swear if you're angry with something or someone, and it doesn't bother you really. It's only what other people think that worries you. I can tell.'

'Well, if I'm your girl,' she glanced at the ring on her finger, 'then I'm entitled to an opinion. It's true what you said, that it doesn't offend me personally – sometimes I find it funny, but sometimes it's embarrassing. Especially when other people are there and it just looks as if you're showing off then. I get embarrassed as much for you as for me, Johnny.'

'OK. But don't start nagging me. Mostly you're a good sport, Annie, but jest because you went to good schools once, don't think you can lord it over us as didn't. Come on, we're wasting our time. If we want to go on the river before we have to meet old Mother Dover then we'll have to be quick.'

'But we can't go – the old boy won't let us have a boat.'

'Who says? He can't watch them all, Annie. Now you do just as I say and we'll have a boat on the river this afternoon – you'll see.'

'What are you going to do, Johnny?'

'Nothing very bad. Nick a boat for half an hour. Now, can you keep him talking, about anything, for five minutes?'

She nodded.

'Right, that'll give me the chance to grab a boat. Look, there's a couple just coming in there. Now while they're talking to him when they get off you be there too, and you get him back into his hut, or at least with his back to the boats see, and then, after five minutes, walk along the bank that way.' He pointed upstream from the boatman's hut, 'and I'll be along there waiting to pick you up.'

'You can row, can't you, Johnny?'

' 'Course I can, silly. I wouldn't think of doing it otherwise. Me and me dad used to always have a boat out on Sunday mornings in the park.'

He left her walking towards the hut, just as the couple in the boat were pulling into the side.

'*Now*, Johnny,' he said to himself when he saw Annie engage the boatman in conversation and start walking towards the hut with him. He was hidden behind a nearby tree and within a minute he had the boat untied and was pulling away from the bank.

He had told Annie the truth when he said he could row, but he had not mentioned that his father or his brothers had always done the bulk of the work, letting him take over for a short while each trip. It was tricky at first, and he needed to get a good way along before he picked Annie up – no use doing it within sight of that old blighter back there.

All went well and when he thought he had travelled far enough Johnny drew in to the side and let the oars rest. He had chosen a good spot, just beyond a weeping-willow tree, which effectively hid the little craft. From here he could watch for her and be ready to pull away once she was safely in the boat.

She came after a while, sauntering along the bank in a casual way and Johnny silently applauded her calm. He whistled softly and saw her look around and hesitate.

'Annie,' he called in a low voice, 'here.'

She ducked beneath the branches of the tree and quickly clambered into the boat. Johnny rowed smartly away.

They hugged the bank for a while longer, then Johnny moved towards the middle of the river. 'We're far enough away now, I think,' he said. 'We should just look like two dots from the hut. Even your plaster won't show up much from this distance.'

Annie looked at it, covered now with signatures and

good-luck messages from her classmates.

'You think of everything, Johnny. Have you done something like this before?'

'No, 'course not. Yes, once me and me brothers did,' he remembered. 'But I was quite small then and didn't have much to do with it. But they had to take me with them because they were supposed to be looking after me that morning.'

'Careful, Johnny.' At Annie's sudden cry he pulled on the oar and managed to miss the other boat, who also took evasive action.

'Think we'll get into the side a bit,' he said, 'but not too much because you can get stuck that way.' From somewhere in his subnconscious memory he recalled hearing his dad say that. It stood him in good stead now and made Annie gaze at him with admiration.

'How far are we going, Johnny?' She looked at her watch. 'We've three-quarters of an hour before we meet Mrs Dover. And we have to return the boat.'

'We'll leave it somewhere along the bank. Maybe where I picked you up,' he said. 'No sense in letting the grumpy old geezer see us now. If he'd let us hire it properly he'd have been paid properly. We'll go on a bit, shall we? It won't take us long to get back.'

They pulled over to the side and Johnny manoeuvred the small craft well. It was all right once you got into the rhythm of the thing, he thought, but it was distracting when they talked. He lost concentration then and they either drifted or started to swing round.

Annie trailed her good hand in the water. 'It's beautiful

out here, isn't it, Johnny. Wish we could stay all day. If we'd come on our own we could have brought our sandwiches and had a picnic on the water.'

'We'll do it another time, shall we? We break up from school next month and can come in more often. Suppose we'd better be getting back now because we'll have to walk along to the café from where we leave the boat.' He started to turn the craft round too quickly and almost collided with another, then the little boat went three times round in circles. Eventually he got over to the bank, but it was the opposite side to where he wanted to be.

'We'll shoot across as soon as there's less traffic,' he said, 'then we'll be all right.'

Johnny was sweating by the time he had manoeuvred the boat across the water. He let the oars rest for a few moments, then he grinned at Annie.

'I'm starving,' he said, 'hope Mrs Dover packed lots of food.'

He started rowing again but he was too close to the bank, so using one oar to push himself away he shot out into mid-river.

Annie laughed. 'I can't wait until my arm's better so I can take a turn rowing with you,' she said. 'You look so powerful.'

'It's easy once you get the knack.' Johnny decided that now they were on the home stretch he'd really dazzle her. He had been a bit bothered getting from one side to the other, but rowing downstream like this now was child's play.

'Hold tight,' he said, 'and we'll go really fast for a few yards before we pull into the side.'

He took a deep breath, grinned at her glowing face, and pulled hard on the oars. Annie gripped one side with her good hand, saw another boat heading for them and stood up, shouting, 'Johnny get out of the way quick.' Then she toppled over into the water.

Johnny jumped in, caught her round the waist and swam with her towards the bank. He was a powerful swimmer and when he reached the bank there was a crowd gathered there to help them both from the water.

'Well done, boy.'

'You both all right.'

'Better get the girl to hospital and let them check that arm, I reckon.'

He heard the comments going on around them, then he saw Mrs Dover. Attracted by the crowd she had walked up to see what was going on.

'Johnny, Anita,' she gasped, 'whatever . . .'

'These two belong to you, missus?'

The man who was even now helping them to their feet looked like a farmer. 'You be a strong swimmer, boy,' he said to Johnny.

'They are my evacuees,' Ethel Dover said.

'Well, best get 'em home and dry 'em out fast. And get the plaster seen to,' he added. 'They'll be none the worse for their soaking, I reckon.'

Mrs Dover saw the boatman first. 'Fancy letting two children go on the river like that,' she said as he approached. 'They could both have drowned. As long as you got your money you didn't bother, I suppose – no sense of responsibility.'

The old man was red in the face as he turned on her. 'Watch your tongue, woman. They stole the boat and if anything had happened no blame could be laid at my door. Unruly children, they ought to be back home where they belong, not causing havoc in our countryside.'

'Stole the boat?'

'Ay, stole it. I did tell 'em they couldn't have it, I did, and next thing the darng boat be gorn and these two here tipping her upside down.'

'We did not tip her upside down,' Johnny said through his shivers. 'We fell out, but we didn't harm the boat.'

'Didn't harm it! When the other boat practically sliced it in two! Look at the damage. Look at it, I say. Young hooligans, and thieves into the bargain.'

'Better get these children home,' someone said. 'Why don't you leave your name and address with the boatman and sort it all out later. The little girl's arm should have attention.'

One of the women in the crowd said she would be happy for them to come to her house and get dry before returning home on the bus, and so the day out finished. They ate their sandwiches, not by the river as planned, but in someone's house in Bushton, wrapped in dressing-gowns that were too big for them, while their clothes flapped about on the washing-line.

It was a grim, silent journey on the bus back to Winchurch, then a trip to the doctor's to check whether Annie would need to return to hospital to have a fresh plaster. It felt soggy and uncomfortable but she knew she would have to put up with that and she didn't expect sympathy.

Johnny was summoned to Mr Dover's study before dinner that evening and when he came out he whispered to Annie, 'Come upstairs as soon as you can.' Then he went to his bedroom. Within five minutes Annie joined him there.

'What happened,' she asked. 'What did he say to you?'

'That I'd have to leave. A long lecture about his own children and how they never behaved like this and he wasn't going to stand it from someone else's when he hadn't had it from his own, blah, blah, blah . . .'

'Leave? Oh no, Johnny. But it isn't fair. It was as much my fault as yours. I'll go and tell him so.'

'No good, Annie. I stole the boat and that's what's got their goat. I don't mind anyway. I've been wanting to go home for ages. Except for leaving you here it's OK by me.'

'Nevertheless I *shall* tell them. I *did* tell them but they wouldn't listen. Well, if you have to go I shall too. Then they'll have no evacuee money at all.'

'I don't think it's much, Annie. And I don't think it would bother them all that much either. They're not poor people, are they?'

Annie didn't answer, and Johnny saw the tears in her eyes. 'Don't start piping yer eye,' he said roughly. 'That's not going to help. And when I'm gone you'll probably forget all about me anyway.'

She shook her head. 'No, I won't. I'll never forget you, Johnny. It's funny really, because if it hadn't been for the war I don't suppose we would have met, would we? I mean I'd have been away at boarding-school and I never came to the places you visited and you never came to mine.'

'I'll miss you,' he said. 'You're not like most girls – you're a good 'un. But it's not the end of everything, Annie. I'll come and visit, they can't stop me doing that, and we'll have a boat out again and go to the pictures and go walking. And when the war's over and you're back in London . . .'

Mrs Dover called up the stairs that dinner was ready. Annie grinned and wiped the tears away. 'You'll forget all about me, I know you will.'

As they reached the top of the stairs he caught hold of her waist. 'I won't, you know. I promise.'

Annie did tell the Dovers that it was as much her fault as Johnny's. 'I egged him on to get the boat,' she lied. 'He wouldn't have taken it on his own, and if that silly old man had let us hire it we wouldn't have taken it at all.'

'That's as may be,' Mrs Dover told her smugly. 'The fact is that Johnny actually took the rowing-boat after he had been told he mustn't have one. He risked both your lives—'

'He saved mine,' she interrupted angrily.

'That's enough, miss. Neither of you should have been on the water in the first place. If you egged him on as you say then you should be ashamed of yourself. And you must be very weak to listen to her,' she said turning to Johnny. 'Anyway our minds are made up. High spirits are one thing – stealing is another. Johnny goes home.'

'Good. You never have wanted me here,' Johnny muttered. 'I'm glad to be going.'

CHAPTER 7

1941

Mrs Bookman had a day off from the factory to come down and sort things out.

'Stealing. Showing us up like that. We may not be as well off as some but you know right from wrong. How *could* you do it, Johnny?'

'Give over, Mum, I didn't pinch his boat. I borrered it for 'alf an hour, that's all.'

'It was stealing, and you could both have drowned . . .'

' 'Cos we wouldn't have,' he interrupted. 'We can both swim.'

'Annie couldn't, with her arm in plaster.'

'I can life-save, can't I? I got a certificate from the baths years ago.'

'Fat lot of good that'd have done. You were lucky, that's all, so don't you let all that praise about saving Annie go to your head, because it was a damn fool thing to do to take the boat like that. The pair of you could have bin sliced in half.'

The train steamed on towards London. Johnny thought how different this was to the way he had dreamed of returning home.

'Another thing,' his mother said, 'I shall have to pay for the repairs to that boat you damaged and you can pay me back each week. You can do a newsround or something.'

'How much will it be?'

'I don't know. You heard what he said, that he'd get an estimate. You should have thought about all that before you stole the thing.'

'You keep going on about stealing the bloo— the boat, but I told you we were going to put it back. We *borrered* it.'

The set of Mrs Bookman's mouth as she said, 'You stole it Johnny, don't split hairs with me,' decided him to keep his thoughts to himself for the rest of the journey.

There was a bonus when they reached home, one he hadn't thought of, for with his brothers both in the army, this time he really did have the bedroom to himself. In any case, he thought, Jim wouldn't be coming back here to live now he was married to Doris, so he'd only be sharing with Ron eventually.

It was strange that he now wanted a bedroom to himself. He recalled the first few nights at the Dovers in what had seemed such a huge room. I 'spect you can get used to things, he thought as he unpacked his case.

'Mum, can I have a box to put Jim and Ron's stuff in?' he called down the stairs.

His mother came up, looking very angry. 'No you

cannot,' she said. 'Jim and Ron are both coming back, please God, and their treasures will be waiting for them.'

'But Mum, I can use the space until they do. And Jim'll have his own place, won't he, now he's married?'

'I said no and I don't want to hear any more about it. Your things are still there waiting for you and theirs will be too. Leave them alone.'

The three boys had a shelf each for their personal belongings. Jim's was the top one as he was the eldest, and originally the tallest; then came Ron's, although from the age of thirteen he had shot up in height and now was bigger than his brother. Johnny's was the lowest one, and was filled with model cars and books. He looked at the books now, after over two years away. They were mostly adventure stories and books about trains and racing-cars. He knew well enough not to try to argue with his mum when she was in such a stubborn mood, and with a great sigh he set about reorganizing what space he had.

'Johnny, hurry up now, I've some bread and dripping here, then we'll go round the school and get you fixed up to start tomorrow.'

Not even a day's holiday from school, he grumbled to himself later that evening when his mum was ironing furiously, and looking very tight-lipped. She put the iron back on to the gas flame for a few seconds, then tested it by holding it up to her face, a practice that had always frightened Johnny. With a shock he realized it still did, and then he understood a little more about his mother's anxiety over what could have happened to him and Annie if they had got into difficulties in the river.

But we didn't, and it's all a lot of fuss over nothing, he thought. If Annie hadn't panicked and stood up suddenly when she saw the other boat coming towards us, then she wouldn't have gone overboard. We *would* have missed the other boat, because I saw it too. He admitted to himself that it was a close thing but they wouldn't have collided. I would have avoided that, I know I would. He didn't hold it against Annie for suddenly standing up. After all, she was more used to horses than boats, he thought, and he would probably do something just as daft and dangerous on a horse.

The return to his old school was an anticlimax. Everyone thought he had simply stopped being evacuated; a lot of the children had returned within months anyway. He no longer belonged to any of the old 'gangs', everything had changed, even the teachers. The only one left whom he knew was the old man they used to call Chubby-Chops because of his resemblance to someone on the films whose cheeks wobbled when he talked and smiled.

His class-teacher was a young woman – well that was OK by him. His previous teacher, Miss Carter, was a young woman and he'd got on all right with her. But this one was different. He sensed her dislike of him straight away, and knew he'd be for it if he didn't watch his step. She had harsh fair hair, hard eyes that stared at you, and she was so skinny.

She picked on him within ten minutes of his arrival because, she said, he wasn't paying attention. Shortly afterwards she moved him to a desk in the front row, 'so I can keep my eyes on you.' By mid-morning he hated her.

He walked home by himself, feeling very miserable. Everything was dowdy – he hadn't remembered the dustiness of the streets, and he hadn't allowed for his old mates who had returned a year and more ago to have formed other friendships. Why, he felt even more of an outsider than he had when he first went to Winchurch. Still, he consoled himself, there were the summer holidays to look forward to in a few weeks, though he didn't know what he'd do if he had no friends to go around with and his mum was out at the factory all day.

Then there was the money he'd have to repay. He saw the prospect of getting the bike he had wanted for so long fast disappearing.

'Poo, bloody poo,' he said loudly, scuffing the toes of his shoes along the kerb.

Annie too felt strange without Johnny around. Mrs Dover fussed her more than usual. 'Is your arm all right? How does it feel, Anita?' Later she said, 'Such a pity you went to London and got injured. Goodness, you could have been killed, my dear, all for the sake of going to the theatre.'

'It was fun. I enjoyed myself,' the girl replied quickly.

'Surely not. It was that young Johnny who persuaded you. I know. He's a charming little rascal when he sets out to be.' She picked up her knitting and smiled across at Annie.

'He didn't have to persuade me, I wanted to go. See a bit of excitement. Oh, the raid was scaring,' Annie said honestly, 'but it wasn't bad really when you read what happens there some nights. We were lucky, and I don't one bit regret going. In fact,' she rushed on, her face flushed now, 'I wouldn't mind going back to London to live, as Johnny has done.'

Mrs Dover pursed her lips tightly together, making all the little wrinkly lines show. 'You ought to be thanking God you are safely here in the country with us, young lady. Bad enough for those who have to be in the thick of it all, but no sense at all in courting danger when there is no need.'

Annie escaped to bed earlier than usual, feigning a great tiredness. Once there she pulled the covers almost over her face and gave herself up to thinking about the last two and a half years. Johnny Bookman had fascinated her from the moment he arrived. His thin, almost haggard-looking face that could suddenly light up with merriment. His speech – she had only heard people speak as Johnny did on the films before, and that not often. Most of all, except when he did it for effect, she loved to hear him say 'Poo, bloody poo' in that throwaway voice. When he did it naturally it never ceased to fill her whole being with laughter. She could feel it bubbling from her toes right through to her head, a delicious, wonderful joy.

She was surprised to find she was crying. 'Stop blubbing,' Johnny would say, 'that don't do no good.' She practised saying it to herself in Johnny's voice and using his grammar, but she only cried more.

Pushing her head well into the pillow for fear of letting the Dovers hear her, she remembered that first night when she had been so lonely until she realized that for Johnny it was worse. Johnny who had never been away from home before, Johnny who was so completely out of his environment that he even called Mrs Dover 'miss'.

'Johnny, Johnny, I wish you hadn't had to go,' she whispered into the pillow. 'It's going to be horrible here without you.'

The following day at school Janet asked Annie to her house to play on Saturday. 'We can mess about in the pool, and take Badger out for a gallop. Will you come?'

The two girls became closer friends after Johnny left and although she wasn't allowed to swim while her arm was in plaster, she could and did go horse-riding. Just a gentle jog through the countryside on a quiet, elderly animal, not a wonderful gallop while her arm was still inactive, but she enjoyed it so.

Sometimes she wondered how Johnny was making out. She wrote to him twice, but had no answers to her letters. Perhaps, after all, Johnny was like everyone else and let you down in the end. Now he was back in his beloved London he had probably forgotten all the good things about Winchurch and Kerry Avenue and the girl he'd bought a ruby ring for.

Annie wore the ring on a slender silver chain around her neck. Never outside her dress or blouse, but always next to her skin. She had taken a small silver cross from the chain so that she could do this and sometimes when she was in her bedroom at night she would slip the ring on to her finger and remember that day in Bushton when Johnny had bought it for her.

Annie had spoken the truth when she told Johnny's mum that her parents were away the weekend she was in

London. It was three and a half weeks later that they caught up with the news. Mrs Dover said privately to her husband, 'I wonder if Anita is really their child, William. They don't bother very much about her, do they? Not underneath the show, I mean. I can't see young Johnny's mum not being in touch for so long, can you?'

'Johnny is no longer our responsibility, Ethel. What he and his parents do or don't do is not our concern now.' As he turned in the bed to give her a perfunctory goodnight kiss, he added in a softer tone, 'I think you're right, though. Go to sleep now, it's late.'

Annie came in from school one day near the end of term as the telephone in the hallway was ringing. Calling out to Mrs Dover, she walked through to the kitchen. There was no one there, but glancing through the window she saw her picking raspberries at the bottom of the garden. She went back to answer the phone herself, something she had never done before.

'Hullo,' a distant voice said, 'is Miss Anita Evesham there? Please,' it added as an obvious afterthought.

'Johnny,' Annie clasped the phone closer, 'Johnny, where are you?'

'Annie. Gosh I didn't think it'd be my luck to have you answer the phone. I'm in a phone-box round the corner from home.'

'Oh Johnny, how are you?'

'I'm all right. How are you?'

'Fine.'

'How's yer arm?'

'It's OK. Johnny, this is a silly conversation. You'll run

out of money. Let's talk properly. Do you miss me?'

'What do you think? 'Course I do. School up here's diabolical.'

'It'll soon be the holidays,' she said, 'maybe we could get together.'

'Let's,' he answered simply. 'Can you come up for a few days? You can have my bed and I'll sleep on the bedchair downstairs.'

'I expect so. Though whether they'll let me after the last time, and the raid, you know what grown-ups are?'

The pips went and she heard more coins go in, then Johnny's voice returned, sounding in a great rush. 'If you can't maybe I'll come down. If I can raise the cash, that is. I have to pay for that bloody boat to be mended.'

'I've got some money, Johnny. You know I never spend all my allowance. We ought to be able to manage something. We could meet half-way perhaps, then no one will know and no one can stop us. Could you get away for long enough?'

'No trouble, Annie. Mum's at the factory all day, and I can always say I'm going to a pal's house for meals.'

The pips went again and Annie heard the clink of money against metal. 'I meant to write,' Johnny said, 'but my letters wouldn't be as good as yours. I reckon I can talk better'n write, y'know.'

Annie laughed delightedly. 'I thought maybe you wanted to forget you'd known me,' she teased.

'Don't be bloody daft,' he said.

Before he rang off they had arranged for Annie to telephone him at the telephone-box on the corner of his road at midday on Saturday. 'I'll have something worked out by then,' she told him, suddenly taking charge, 'but we'll need to be careful because if they find out they'll all probably try to stop us meeting.'

Longing to tell someone, she didn't trust Janet enough to confide in her, so she whispered the news to Podge, her fat teddy-bear when they were snuggled into the bedclothes that night.

She had a strange dream that night too. She dreamt she had run away from the Dovers, but instead of going home, in case her people weren't there she went to Johnny's house. Mrs Bookman said she could stay, and although at first she jumped at the chance it didn't work out. They were kind but they lived in a totally different way from her and she wasn't sure she could live like it for always. She woke up as she was running out of their front door, and she was crying.

When she rang Johnny on Saturday she had it worked out and written down. She told him the train times, and how she had arranged it with Janet to say that she was going with her and her family on an outing, should anyone question her. 'Can you meet the train, Johnny?'

'I'll be there, Annie.'

'Good. I know the times coming back. I mustn't be too late. That's why I'm coming very early.'

She hadn't actually told Janet whom she was meeting, just that it was important for her to be away for the day. She had hinted that she would tell her the whole story soon, and had sworn her to secrecy about the whole thing.

She had a lighter plaster on her arm now, but it was still

a nuisance to her for she couldn't play tennis, could only have gentle rides instead of exhilarating gallops, and couldn't swim. The only bright prospect for the summer holidays was being able to see Johnny again, and she knew she would have to play that one carefully or there would be more trouble, and possibly no further meetings. Then, she thought, the future would be bleak indeed.

Saturday was warm and sunny, and Annie, who had woken at 5.30 and forced herself to stay in bed until 6.45, dressed in a lime-green cotton frock which she knew brought out chestnut gleams in her dark-brown hair. She gazed at herself in the mirror and hoped Johnny would find she was pretty.

Mrs Dover came into the kitchen while she was eating her toast. 'Just to make sure you get away all right, Anita,' she said. 'We must be very quiet and not disturb Mr Dover.'

Annie stifled a smile as she thought that by herself there would have been no noise at all, whereas now, with Mrs Dover chattering to her, 'the master' as she and Johnny had privately nicknamed him, could well be woken up.

She left the house in plenty of time to catch the five past eight train. Mrs Dover had remarked on this several times during the week. 'It would cost less if you went after nine, Anita dear.' And her answer was always the same, 'Well, Mummy and Daddy are paying and they want me to be there early.'

It was a good job Mummy and Daddy never came to see her and as far as she knew had no contact with the Dovers either. There would be trouble if she was found out, of course, maybe not so much with her parents, but certainly with her foster-parents.

Johnny was at the station to meet her, looking very smart in long grey-flannel trousers and an open-necked blue shirt. His dark hair gleamed – she thought he must have used some of his dad's Brylcreem on it. He took both her hands in his as she came through the barrier. 'Gosh, I kept wondering if you'd be on the train after all,' he said.

'I told you I would.'

'I know, Annie, but someone might have stopped you. Anyway, what do you want to do?'

'I don't mind. Just walk and talk and have fun. I've got some money with me so we can have something to eat when we're hungry.'

'So have I, Annie and it'll be my treat. I've got a job.'

'A real job?'

' 'Course. After school I help in a shop near us. I'm not allowed to serve – too young or something, but I'm sort of general dogsbody. I think you have to be fourteen really, and I'm only twelve but the woman who runs it needs someone young and strong to lift things sometimes, so she turns a blind eye 'cos I'm useful to her. I fill up the shelves when the stock arrives, and count the coupons and get them ready to go to the authorities. It's quite interesting really, and I get paid, see. Then there's me morning news-paper-round too, so even with paying me mum back for damage to that old bugger's boat I've got some left to spend.'

'You are a goer, aren't you, Johnny? I bet nothing ever beats you.' He looked uncomfortable. 'She wanted me

Saturdays too, the woman in the shop, but I wouldn't do it, so I can see you then. Come on,' he said, 'let's have an ice-cream to start with while we decide where we're going.'

It was the first of many Saturday outings for them. Annie invented a cousin who lived in London, and while it didn't satisfy Mrs Dover's curiosity there was nothing she could do about it. In case she was ever tempted to check with Mrs Evesham Annie told her mother in a letter that a great friend of hers at school had an aunt whom she visited each week and she usually went with her.

'Then if they do get together on my story any time I'll be for it, of course, but if they don't, then they both think they know where I am each Saturday. Except of course that I'm not.' She giggled and Johnny, looking awestruck, said, 'You are so good at this sort of thing Annie.'

Johnny was allowed to keep his earnings once he had given his mother something for the repairs to the damaged boat, and he used it for his fare and spending-money each Saturday. Annie wanted to pay this for him because she knew she had more than he did, 'and it was as much my fault as yours,' she argued, but he always refused.

'The day I'm skint I'll tell you,' he said. 'Now let's enjoy ourselves.'

They walked and talked, went to newsreels, cartoons, pictures, even once a matineé at the theatre, and that meant Annie had to catch a later train back. She telephoned the Dovers to say she would be late, inventing a friend who had called unexpectedly and invited them for tea.

They pooled their money once each had paid their train fare, and apart from a sandwich or some crisps and Tizer it didn't cost much because when they went to the cinema it was always at the front in the ninepennys.

Each time they parted Johnny said, 'Next Saturday, Annie?'

'Next Saturday, Johnny.'

CHAPTER 8

1943

'Mummy's coming down tomorrow, Johnny,' Annie said one Saturday when they met at their usual rendezvous. This wasn't the only meeting-place, but was the one they used most because it was about halfway for them both and they could get on a train to town or to various other places from that station.

'What's she coming for, Annie?'

'Apparently to discuss my future.'

'She's not taken much notice of it for the last few years,' said Johnny. 'I suppose now you're coming up to earning-age she wants to know.'

'I don't think it's that.' Annie frowned. 'They're not hard up are they? I think they'll probably want me to go on with my education. I mean if the war wasn't on I would have gone to finishing school in Switzerland or something like that in a year or so.'

'Blimey Annie, would you really?'

She nodded. 'Anyway you couldn't get to Switzerland now, could you, even though it's neutral?'

'I s'pose not.'

'She might make me go to her sister in America. I don't want to, Johnny. I just want to stay here and go out to work.'

'Well tell her that. She can't force you to do it. Not now you're nearly fourteen she can't. And if you don't want to go you'll simply be unhappy and it will be like the board- ing school over again. I think it should be your decision, not your parents.'

'If I went to one in this country it wouldn't be so bad,' she went on as though she hadn't heard him. 'I'd have more freedom than at the Dovers.'

'You know, Annie, it's amazing we get on so well because we're poles apart really.'

They were heading for their favourite café 'Are we, Johnny?'

'You just said that if it hadn't been for the war you'd have gone to Switzerland or somewhere to finishing- school. Then I suppose you'd have been married off to some rich bloke—'

'Hey, steady on. Mummy and Daddy had a bit of a struggle at first, I think, to keep me at that school and I owe them something. But not that. I'd never let them marry me off, Johnny. When the time comes I shall choose the man I'll marry.'

'Good for you. But in the normal way we would never

have met and been friends, would we? When I left school I'd have gone with my dad on the barrow. That's what both my brothers did before they got their own patch. Now I'll go into the army, unless the war's over before I'm seventeen.'

Annie smiled at him, thinking how nicely he talked now and how smart he looked and knowing that the essential Johnny, the one who made her laugh and who looked after her and for whom she was willing to risk the wrath of her parents, the Dovers, or anyone else who tried to come between them, was still there.

'What about us, Johnny?' she said.

'What d'you mean?'

'Well, we'll both be old enough to leave school soon. I might have to go on, though I didn't take the scholarship. I thought that I would suggest a shorthand-and-typewriting course – I'd prefer that to learning to be a lady.'

'I should just think you would.'

'What will you do?'

'Get a job until I go in the army.'

'The war's not going to last for ever, Johnny.'

'No, and when it's over I'm going to have some fun. Both of us will, I hope.'

'Together,' she murmured.

'Of course. If you haven't married some rich bloke.'

'I shan't do that,' she said quietly.

They went into the café. The proprietor knew them well now and smiled cheerfully at them. He brought their Tizer and said, 'A special treat today because you two are such regular customers. *Voilà*,' and he placed in front of them two large cream horns.

'On the house,' he said. 'Enjoy them.'

'Gosh, wasn't it sweet of that old man,' Annie said when they were outside in the sunshine again. 'I suppose we have been coming here a lot.'

'Mmm,' Johnny replied.

'Will you still want to come when you have a job?'

' 'Course. Might not be able to, though, if I have to work Saturdays.'

'Maybe I could come on up to town and meet you there and we could go out in the evenings,' said Annie.

'D'you think you could get away with it, Annie?'

'Well, we're hardly children any more. Least, you'll be earning, and if I can get myself into an office somewhere so shall I. Come to that I could work in London, couldn't I?'

'That would make things easier. It's funny, isn't it, Annie – we were both evacuated so as we'd be safe, and now I'm back living up here and you come up every week.'

'Mmm. Where does your mum think you go on Saturdays, Johnny?'

'Out with me mates. I never actually say. What was the word old man Dover was so fond of— yes, specific, specifically. Sometimes she asks leading questions, but I always fob her off.'

'Would she mind, do you think? You and me meeting, I mean?'

He shrugged. 'Why should she?'

'No reason,' Annie answered quickly, 'but you know what grown-ups are?'

Annie always wore the ring Johnny had bought her on

her finger on Saturdays when they met, but during the week at school it stayed comfortingly on the silver chain around her neck.

'Still got it,' he said now, awkwardly taking hold of her hand.

'Mmm. It's pretty.'

'So are you, Annie. I've always thought so. Prettier than any other girl in the school.'

She squeezed his fingers in appreciation, and he let go of her hand so suddenly she laughed. 'Sorry, Johnny, did I hurt you?'

'No, 'course not.' He touched her clumsily. 'What would you like to do today?'

'Go to Buckingham Palace.'

Afterwards she wondered whatever had induced her to say that. She had seen the palace before, several times, yet once the words were out she felt excited at the thought.

'Don't expect the King and Queen are there, but come on, then, and afterwards we'll go and feed the pigeons in Trafalgar Square, shall we?'

They returned to the station for the next train into town. It was crowded, soldiers, sailors and airmen of all nationalities, WAAFS, ATS and WRENS as well as a smattering of the civilian population.

'I should like to go in the Wrens when I leave school,' Annie said, 'but you have to be seventeen, I checked. That's why I thought about a job in London for a few years . . .'

'Seems funny to think of you in a uniform,' said Johnny.

'You know how I always think of you before I go to sleep at night?'

She held her breath. 'No Johnny, how?'

He bent his head low, so it was almost touching her shoulder and he didn't look at her face as he said, 'In that pink dressing-gown, and your hair all loose and hanging round your shoulders. You looked like a film star, Annie, honest you did.'

The train jerked to a stop and they both shot forward. They were nearly into the station, and Johnny was glad of the chance to change the subject. He hadn't meant to say anything along those lines to Annie, they were his night-time thoughts, and sometimes his dreams.

'Wonder what we've stopped for?' he said loudly, and at that moment they started again, puffing steadily into the terminus.

On the platform a couple of American airmen went by and gave them a friendly grin. Johnny felt for her hand. 'I could lose you in this crowd otherwise,' he said, his face flushed. She smiled at him as she returned the pressure.

Both knew their way about London well, Johnny possibly better than Annie. She knew the monuments and famous buildings, and he knew these and lots of smaller interesting places too. Alleys that led to elegant squares where they sometimes walked, gazing at the houses.

'Aren't they wonderful?' Annie would say. 'Can't you imagine them when people wore crinolines and horse-drawn carriages pulled up outside to take sir and madam for a drive or to the pleasure-gardens?'

Johnny didn't know about the pleasure-gardens, but he

listened to Annie and asked questions and one week she brought up a library book about them. He was fascinated.

'Reckon I could have worked in a place like that, Annie,' he said when he returned it the following week, 'and you'd have been the fine lady who came to watch and buy.'

But today they headed for Buckingham Palace. They weren't surprised to find a small crowd gathered there, many in uniform, but to their great delight within minutes of their arrival the policeman on the gate strode forward and held up the traffic to allow a large black car through. It happened very quickly, and they had a wonderful view of the King and Queen and two princesses.

'Golly, gosh,' Annie said, 'that's the very first time I've seen them except on the newsreels. Weren't they lovely? Princess Elizabeth was nearest to me and she looked right into my eyes. Gosh, Johnny I'm so thrilled I – I think I'm going to cry.'

'Aw, don't cry, Annie, not with all these people about. You liked seeing them, didn't you?'

'Yes, of course I did.' She looked at him with shining eyes. 'How lucky we were, Johnny. Just that very moment.'

'I've never seen them before either,' he said. 'They're more beautiful than their photographs, aren't they?'

'Mmm. Such blue eyes the princesses have. Oh Johnny, what a perfect day. Shall we go to Trafalgar Square now?'

They turned from the palace gates and almost bumped into a lady and gentleman who gazed at them with amazement showing clearly in their faces.

'Anita. What are you doing here?'

'Mummy.'

Johnny found the next few minutes very confusing indeed. Annie touched his arm and he could feel her hand trembling. 'Johnny, these are my mother and father,' she said.

He held out his hand. 'How do you do.'

'This is Johnny Bookman,' Annie told them.

Mrs Evesham barely acknowledged him, but Annie's father held out his hand too. 'Glad to know you, Johnny,' he said.

'What on earth are you doing m London, Anita?'

'Well, Mummy . . .' She drew a deep breath, trying frantically to find the right words.

'Anita, I'm waiting. I want the truth. Why aren't you in Winchurch or Bushton – wherever it is you go on a Saturday?'

Johnny burst in then. 'I can explain that, Mrs Evesham. I asked Annie to come to London with me today.'

'You did?' The scorn in her voice made Johnny wince.

'Yes, I did.' He strove to keep his tone low, smothering his natural indignation at being spoken to in that manner. 'Annie is a friend of mine and I invited her out for the day.'

He thought Mrs Evesham was going to burst wide open. She seemed to swell all over, her face grew rounder and pinker, she waved her arms about, and she looked just like a barrage-balloon about to break from its moorings.

'Look, Mummy, I can explain . . .' but Annie's mother didn't allow her to get any further.

'You'll have to, my girl, you'll have to. Come along.'

'Oh, I say, Eunice, let the young people have their chance. How about a cup of tea somewhere and we can sort this out.'

Johnny warmed to Annie's dad, but Mrs Evesham was tugging at Annie now, and she shot her husband a look of such venom that Johnny wasn't surprised when he said quietly, 'You had better come with your mother, Anita.'

Annie touched Johnny's arm gently. 'Might be better if I do,' she whispered.

'But . . .' Already Mrs Evesham was almost dragging Annie away.

'They could force me, Johnny,' she hissed, 'and you'd be in trouble too.'

'I don't know what your parents are about,' was Mrs Evesham's parting shot to Johnny, 'but I'll warrant they don't know about this. Wandering about London at your ages and in these times. . . .' She hustled her husband and Annie away, and Johnny stood there afterwards and wondered whether he was dreaming and would suddenly wake up and find himself in bed instead of outside Buckingham Palace, where the gold of the day had suddenly turned to grey. He was standing there still when Annie broke away and rushed back.

'Next week, Johnny – I'll be there.' She turned and slowly, with great dignity, walked back to where her parents were waiting.

Johnny went home. His thoughts were all of Annie. She was certainly some girl. It took courage to defy her parents, especially that old dragon of a mother. He felt a surge of gratitude that his mother wasn't like that.

On his way back he saw nothing of his surroundings, his thoughts were all for Annie. What would happen to her?

What would her parents do to her? He berated himself for not being able to protect her – if only he was a few years older it couldn't have happened, he thought, but she was still a minor and neither she nor he would have a leg to stand on if anyone decided to part them.

He was so worried he almost went past his bus-stop. The clippie smilingly chided him for day-dreaming when he jumped up as she had her hand to the bell.

His sister-in-law Doris and her mother were there when he got home. He had forgotten this was his mother's Saturday off – she worked two out of three.

'You're early,' she said.

'Yes.' He walked through to the hall to go upstairs to his bedroom.

'Where've you been?' she said.

'Out.' His voice was belligerent.

'Johnny. I asked you a civil question and I expect a civil answer. Where have you been?'

'Messing around.'

'You said you were going to someone's house for dinner and tea. You haven't been sent home, have you?'

He held back the words that sprang to his lips, and glancing at Doris and her mother he said, 'Mum thinks I'm still a little boy in short pants.'

'Never mind what I think.' She came and stood in front of him, so he would have to look her in the face. 'You made a point of saying not to save dinner or tea for you today because you were going to be at some boy's house – Dave's, wasn't it? all day. It's half past three, so what happened?'

'For crying out loud, Mum. Do I have to account for my movements as though I'm a criminal? I didn't stay as long, that's all. No reason, I just didn't.' He slammed out of the room.

He heard the babble of talk as he entered his bedroom, but he was left in peace. He flung himself on to the bed and swore.

Over half an hour later he heard sounds downstairs and realized that Doris and her mother were leaving. Now he'd be for it. He wished he'd kept his mouth shut, but his mother's questioning had been the last straw in a day that had begun so well and finished so badly. And he was worried over Annie. What if they beat her?

'Johnny.'

He straightened himself up, flexed his muscles to try and make them ripple as he remembered the strong man at the fair used to do. During the time he had been upstairs he had worked out what he hoped was a plausible story. No use telling his mother that he and Annie met every Saturday – not now, it wasn't. She'd be sure to kick up about it because it had been going on for so long without her knowing. And at the back of his mind was the fact that if she banned them from meeting, it would mean either never seeing Annie again, or telling more lies.

With a certainty he had never before experienced he knew which he'd opt for. Annie was the girl he would marry when they were both old enough. He loved her like his dad loved his mum and together they would be a great team. Unless she did marry someone else, but only if that someone was her choice. He would have to accept it then.

Johnny didn't want to lie to his mum, but it seemed to him it was the lesser of two evils. This was a phrase she herself often used, so maybe she would understand his predicament if she found out later. Best to tell one lie now about today and hope she left it at that so he wouldn't need to do it again.

She had her 'no-nonsense' face on when he entered the room. In fact, he thought, her whole bearing was the same.

'I want the truth, Johnny. You didn't go to Dave's or anyone else's today. So where were you and what were you doing?'

He looked towards the floor.

'Well, Johnny. Start talking.'

'We had a fight. Now don't get it wrong – it was outside. Several of us, so we simply didn't go to Dave's house.'

'Look at me, Johnny?'

He looked up quickly.

'I see. So where did you go instead?'

'Oh just around. The park, the common.'

'Do I know this Dave? Is he from round here?'

'He – he lives the other side of the park, in Benstead Road. I told you when I went there once before.'

'That's right, so you did. I'd forgotten. Well, bring him round here one Saturday when I'm off, Johnny.'

'Is that all. Can I go now?'

'Yes, except I'm going out tonight with some of the girls from the factory. Your dad's firewatching and as I thought you'd be having dinner and tea with your friend Dave I haven't cooked anything. Better get yourself some chips from Mrs Joe on the corner. I'll give you some money.'

Johnny suddenly realized how very hungry he was. Since the cream horn in the café this morning he'd had nothing to eat or drink.

'Thanks, Mum. Sorry I snapped, but you did make me look a fool in front of Doris and her mum. Sometimes I don't think you realize how old I am. Soon I'll be out at work proper and you won't be able to tell me what to do then.'

'We'll see. All the while you're in this house you'll do as your dad and I say. We're older than you and we know best. Now listen, I won't be late this evening – if the warning goes get under the Morrison table and stay there. Understand.'

'Yes mum,' he said in an exaggerated tone.

'And watch yourself, Johnny. Liars always get found out.'

CHAPTER 9

1943

Annie fought back tears as she went with her parents. No further word was spoken until they reached a bus-stop. There was a queue and her mother said crossly, 'Almost impossible to get a taxi and the buses are so crowded.'

She had her arm firmly tucked into her daughter's although she seemed to be addressing her remarks to nobody in particular. Then suddenly she turned her face towards Annie's. 'You had better watch your step, Anita. Running after a boy like that.' She pulled her lips together in a thin, disapproving line.

The girl and her father kept silent. When she saw their bus approaching Annie said, 'I have to get back to Winchurch.'

'Oh no, you are coming back with us tonight. I shall telephone Mrs Dover and find out about a few things. And you have some explaining to do. We want to know exactly what has been going on.'

'Nothing's been going on. Johnny and I simply had a day out. Nothing to make such a fuss over.'

Mrs Evesham gripped her arm tighter and almost pushed her on to the bus. 'We will discuss the matter at home, not in public if you don't mind,' she said.

By the time they reached home Annie had conquered her tearfulness and was simply feeling rebellious.

'You're treating me like a child,' she said. 'We were doing no wrong and you were extremely rude to Johnny.'

'That's enough. I knew we should not have allowed you to be evacuated with the rest. I wanted you to go to my sister in America, but no, that wasn't right for your father.'

Half-turning towards her husband she said bitterly, 'I should never have listened to you. Look at the result of your great idea now. Our daughter mixing with boys like that one this afternoon. What are you going to do about that?'

'We don't know the lad, do we? He may be—'

'That is not the point,' his wife interrupted; her voice sharp with anger and anxiety. 'Anita is still only fourteen and we thought she was safely in the country. Mrs Dover has something to answer for here. Where did you tell her you were going today?' She turned back to her daughter.

'All right, I'm completely in the wrong. I admit it. I told her I was having a day out with a friend. That was the truth, but I didn't tell her it was in London in case she wouldn't let me go.'

'So. Did she not ask where you were going?'

Annie thought quickly. If she landed Mrs Dover in too

much trouble she might have to come back here to live.

'Yes, she did actually, and I'm afraid I lied to her.'

Mrs Evesham closed the door while she telephoned Mrs Dover. Anita and her father sat opposite each other and listened to the muted sounds from the hall. Then he smiled at her. 'How many times have you had a day out with young Johnny, Anita?' he asked softly.

'Q-quite a lot,' she said.

'He is also billeted with the Dovers, isn't he?'

'He used to be. He came back to London two years ago.'

Mrs Evesham returned. 'I have told the Dovers I shall bring you back myself tomorrow. We were coming down then anyway to talk about your future. I shall have quite a bit to say to them, too, about allowing you to run loose. I won't have it. They take money for looking after you and I expect the job to be properly done. If she can't do it, then we will find somewhere else. What is that on your finger? Show me.' She pulled Annie's hand towards her as the girl made to cover Johnny's ring with her other hand.

'A ring. And you're wearing it on your engagement finger. You silly little fool, what sort of game do you and that stupid boy think you're playing?'

She tugged at her daughter's finger and, red-faced and with tears spilling over now, Annie resisted with all her might.

'Leave it alone, it's mine.'

'I suppose he gave it to you. A cheap bit of jewellery—'

'Leave it alone, leave it alone,' Annie screamed, 'you don't know what you're talking about.' She wrenched her hand from her mother's grasp, and sobbing uncontrollably, rushed out of the room and upstairs.

It was Mr Evesham who tapped on her door an hour later. 'Anita, may I come in?' he called softly.

She was calmer then, and already making plans. She knew there wasn't anything she could do until tomorrow, but somehow she had to smooth things over sufficiently to enable her to stay in Winchurch a few months longer until she was fourteen. Until then they could force her home, but after that, she thought, I can be independent.

'Anita, your mother was worried, that's why she carried on. She's very fond of you, and it was a great shock to her to see you in London with a young boy when she thought you were safely in the country.'

She had put the ring away in her purse, not risking it round her neck even, where the silver chain would show in the V of her summer-frock.

'We weren't doing any harm and she didn't give us a chance to explain.'

'Well, you know your mother, Anita. Listen, I've persuaded her to leave it until tomorrow, when we go to Winchurch and sort everything through. Meanwhile you must be hungry, so come downstairs and have some tea with us and let it simmer down a while. Come on, what do you say?'

'All right, Dad.' She found her voice was trembling with tears still. 'I'll just go and and clean up a bit.' She brushed her hand across her eyes.

'Good girl. Don't be too long, will you?'

Annie had often suspected that if it came to a real crisis between her and her mother she would have her father's backing. She often wished she could get to know him better, but she had been at home so little during her life, and then it was always her mother who was dominant. He had obviously intervened on her behalf now, with success. Well, she could play a waiting game. Once she was back with the Dovers, although her movements would probably, almost certainly be curtailed she could contact Johnny and make plans for when she left school. What sort of plans she didn't yet know, but if she could get a job and earn some money, then she didn't think her mother would enforce the law to make her live at home.

The atmosphere was not convivial, but her mother accepted the truce. Neither Johnny nor the ring were mentioned, although Annie saw her mother's eyes look at her bare fingers. She was amazed to discover how hungry she was once she began eating. Guiltily, she thought she shouldn't feel ravenous like this when she was so unhappy. Resolutely she pushed away her images of Johnny and what he might be doing at this minute. She wanted to be clear-headed now for the battle that, in spite of the current calmness, was still in progress.

After tea they listened in silence to the wireless. Mrs Evesham knitted steadily throughout, and Annie wished she too had something to prevent her hands from fidgeting.

The set was turned up for the nine o'clock news and Annie listened as they talked of Kasserine and the Mareth Line, strange sounding names to her. She watched various expressions flit across her father's face as he spread a well-worn map across the table by the side of his chair, and study it intensely. The only sound apart from the news-reader's voice was the even click of her mother's knitting needles. As soon as the news bulletin was over, her father switched the set off. He glanced down at the map, then across to his daughter, and for a moment she thought he was going to discuss it with her, but he just smiled and settled back into his chair. Annie looked at her mother.

'I'll – get off to bed,' she said.

'Everything is as you left it,' Mrs Evesham said, without a pause in her knitting.

Annie went upstairs.

She opened the drawer of the chest in her room, took out one of the nightdresses and thought how strange it was to be back in this bedroom tonight. If anyone had asked her this morning where she would be this evening, the last place she would have thought about was here. The idea gave her courage, for if this turn of events could happen so suddenly and unexpectedly, who knew what might happen in a few more days, or another week, or month?

'Goodnight Johnny,' she whispered, her hands clasped round the ring, back on her finger for the night.

The journey to Winchurch and the meeting with the Dovers were as distressing as Annie suspected they would be. But, back in her own room in Kerry Avenue that night, she consoled herself with the knowledge that she had won a reprieve. There had been much anger and wringing of hands between her mother and Mrs Dover and, as she had known would happen, she came in for her share of blame. 'Lying to meet a boy ...'

'It is not entirely Anita's fault.' Mrs Dover actually stuck up for her. 'Johnny Bookman is a persuasive boy, he has a certain . . .' she seemed at a loss for the right word for a moment, then she said, 'a certain way with him . . . *almost* a charm. . . .'

Annie nearly laughed. She must remember this to tell Johnny. She imagined his reaction.

'Poo, bloody poo,' he'd probably say.

How stupid they all were, she thought many hours later when she was in bed, Johnny's ring once more on her finger. Normally she took it off from round her neck, still on its chain, and laid it on the dressing-table ready for the morning, but tonight she wore it again, just to be sure.

The ring had not been mentioned again, either to her or to Mrs Dover. On the whole she had got off lightly, she thought, pushing away the idea that it was only because her mother didn't want to be bothered with her at home that she had been allowed back here to Winchurch. The feelings of being unwanted hurt her, perhaps even more now that she was older, but she was grateful not to have been sent anywhere else. If that had happened she could have been too far away for the weekly trips.

She thought over some of the things that had been said. Tighter restrictions; that wasn't so good. She would have to work out a really sound plan now to be able to escape on Saturday. She would need proof to show Mrs Dover where she was going, and if she was to get to London to meet Johnny she would have to think of something.

She thought of it on the way to school on Monday morning. Janet was her answer, surely. They were good friends, and if Janet would help her then the meetings could continue until she left school and went to London to work. It would mean confiding in Janet of course, but that couldn't be helped. She would have to do it.

Not wishing to waste time she asked Janet at playtime. 'Can I talk to you privately, Janet?' she said, 'it's rather important.'

'Sure, Annie.' They all called her Annie at school now since Johnny had started the fashion.

She told Janet about the weekend and its result. 'So you see, Janet, I need to go on Saturday because I promised. And I want to. But Johnny will be terribly worried if I don't turn up. He'll probably ring through to the Dovers to try and talk to me and I'm sure they won't let him. My mother gave them such a roasting I'm surprised they kept me on, really I am.'

'I'll help you,' Janet said. 'I'd love to. We must be very careful though. We'll draw up a plan for each week. It mustn't be the same thing every time because that will arouse their suspicion.'

'Janet, you are a sport. And my very best friend.'

It was several days before the girls had worked out what they were going to do. Then Annie wrote to Johnny to tell him. Janet and Annie were going to the railway station together – in fact Janet was even going to call for Annie. She would travel two stations, to Bushton, have a look round the shops and then return home, but Annie would stay on the train to meet Johnny and everything would be as normal.

Of course, she wrote, *we shall have to vary this a bit because*

141

*Janet won't want to go into Bushton every week, and this in itself
will arouse suspicion. But for this week I will be there an hour
later than usual because we think it unwise to leave too early.*

On Friday night Mrs Evesham telephoned. That was
unusual, and it made Annie realize even more that she
would need to be very careful and devious if they were not
to be found out. The thought of being discovered and
stopped appalled her. Johnny might just shrug his shoulders and not bother any more. She didn't think he would,
but he might. . . .

He was waiting by the ticket-barrier when she arrived
on Saturday.

'Gosh, Annie, am I glad to see you. Was it awful? She
didn't hurt you, did she?'

'No, not physically anyway. But it was dreadful bad
luck, wasn't it, bumping into them like that?' He nodded
his head vigorously. 'How about you, Johnny, how did you
get on?'

'Bit of a barney with me mum, but we soon sorted it out.
I didn't tell her where I'd been or who I was with, of
course.'

'Johnny,' she touched his arm, 'would your mum mind
so much, do you think? I mean, if I can get a job in London
when I leave school in a few weeks it will be easier if we
can meet openly, won't it?'

'I suppose so, Annie, but, oh heck, I don't know. See, I'm
going to marry you some day – that is if you'll have me of
course, and, well I don't think grown-ups understand that
sort of thing.'

'Johnny.' She stopped so suddenly he was still walking

on, and she ran to catch him up. 'Was that a – a proposal, Johnny?'

'Now don't go all funny on me, Annie. I guess it was, really. I don't want any other girl but you, but it'll be years 'n' years before we can do anything about it.'

'I know,' she said, 'and you're absolutely right, we have to be practical. But I – I accept Johnny. I'll marry you when we're older and are earning some money. I've got some savings too.'

'Well, we can talk about it in a few years' time, when the war's over and everything. I've been thinking about you all week, Annie. Come on, we'll get a fizzy drink. Bet he won't give us cream horns again this week.' Their fingers touched as they both ran down the road to the café.

Their arrangements for meeting worked well, but they now varied the venue more. Because Johnny was a freer agent and could leave as early as he needed to, he sometimes travelled further from London now to meet her. Janet stuck to her part of the bargain with Annie and always provided an excuse for her to be gone all day. This didn't easily fool Mrs Dover, who asked many searching questions of Annie and, when she had the opportunity, of Janet too. But as she did not know Janet's parents, and as the girl refused all invitations to Kerry Avenue, this was more difficult, Annie's plan couldn't be checked on.

Annie had bought a riding-hat and jodhpurs in Bushton, carefully requesting the money from her parents and making a great point of the number of times she rode Janet's sister's horse, Flash, and borrowed her gear. She kept these at Janet's house, their supposed riding activities provided the best excuse for being out all day, and sometimes Annie wished she really was going riding with Janet. I'll teach Johnny to ride when we are married, she thought.

She dreamed of her wedding to Johnny one day in the future, maybe when I'm nineteen or twenty, she thought, and she hugged the knowledge of his love to herself. Not that he had actually said: 'I love you, Annie,' but then she didn't expect him to. He had asked her to marry him, and she relived that moment in the deserted street often, and treasured the memory.

Janet sometimes asked what they did all day. 'Can't be much fun being out with a boy like Johnny,' she said once. 'I mean, he's not exactly tall, dark and handsome, is he?'

'I don't like tall, dark, handsome men,' Annie replied, without any knowledge of men at all, 'and there's much more to Johnny than you would imagine from his appearance. He's very quick-witted, tremendous fun, ever so kind. Johnny wouldn't hurt a fly, however he carries on. And he doesn't swear now – well, only occasionally when he's sort of thrown off balance.'

On the few occasions when Annie did actually go riding she enjoyed it tremendously, and one Sunday a few weeks later the girls took a packed lunch and set off with the horses.

After an exhilarating gallop over the moor and a leisurely lunch, they quietly made their way home. They were in the lane leading back to Winchurch when a car raced past. Startled, both horses became skittish, but the girls calmed them and went on. Within a few seconds there was another car, then came one at normal speed, which did slow down, then, as both girls acknowledged the courtesy, another car rushed past them and Flash reared, unseating Annie and throwing her into the ditch.

She lay there stunned for several seconds, then someone leapt in and crouched down beside her. She heard Janet's voice faintly in the distance, then a man said, 'We'll have you out of there in a moment. Can you move your limbs?' His hand reached for the back of her neck, and gently felt her all over. 'Nothing seems to be broken so give me your hands and I'll help you up.'

Annie's first concern was for Flash, but Janet, looking pale and shaken, and holding her horse's reins said she would go after him now she knew Annie wasn't badly injured and needing an ambulance. Sitting on the verge and feeling bruised and battered but relieved to be in one piece, Annie said, 'It was those cars, they must have been having a race or something. They whizzed by. Flash is a docile and steady horse usually, very placid. I do hope he's all right.'

'Your friend has gone after him. I'm Doctor Morgan from Bushton. Once I have checked you over properly I'll contact the police; those madmen were escaping from something. They tore past me, but when I reached you your animals were fine, then suddenly the third car came up behind. I suspect he was one of them. I suddenly saw him in my mirror and looked back to see you go into the ditch. Now, do you think you can make it to the car or would you like me to carry you over?'

'I can make it,' she said. 'It's so kind of you. Are you on your way to a patient, though?'

'No. I've just left one, so there's no urgency. I'll take you home first.'

'But Flash—'

'I'll go and look for your friend once you are safely back.'

She directed him to Janet's house. As they approached they saw Janet leading both horses through the gate leading into the field. Tears ran down Annie's cheeks with the relief of knowing the horse was unhurt and back in his field. Dr. Morgan took her home to Kerry Avenue, where, with Mrs Dover as chaperon, he examined her in the privacy of her bedroom. She was feeling pretty tender and sore by then, but the doctor said she had bruised her ribs and would suffer pain from this for several weeks, but that everything was in place and no lasting damage had occurred. He telephoned the police station from the Dovers' house before accepting a cup of tea and going on his way.

The accident did have one good point because it convinced her parents and the Dovers that she really did go riding with Janet. She felt guilty about her deceit, but if it was a question of seeing Johnny or not seeing Johnny, then there was no choice for her.

On the Saturday she went off to meet him as usual, and this time a visit to Janet's cousin was again her excuse for being away all day. She felt very stiff although she pretended she wasn't.

Johnny was filled with concern. She couldn't hide her pain from him, having winced when he greeted her with a hug.

'I hope they catch those bloody crooks,' he said, 'they could have maimed you for life or even killed you. God, Annie, it don't bear thinking about. If the horse had gone in the ditch with you he would have crushed you—'

'But he *didn't*, Johnny, and, apart from some aches and pains for a few weeks I'm fighting fit. And I have already started looking round for a job for when I leave school. If I can't find something in Winchurch I'll try Bushton. Come on now, tell me all your news. How's your mum and dad? Any news from your brothers? And what are we going to do today?'

Gently he put his hand up to her hair and, with infinite tenderness, stroked it rhythmically, 'Whatever you want to. But no running and jumping, that I forbid today.'

'Poo, bloody poo,' she answered, and although it hurt her like mad, she was glad to see the worry disappear from his face as they both rocked with laughter.

CHAPTER 10

1943

Johnny had settled into a routine again after a few months back at his London school. Gradually he infiltrated the groups in his class and was accepted.

There was a bit of bawdy teasing when word got around that he was seeing a girl at the weekends, and he countered this with a few saucy jokes and an attitude that they were simply jealous because he seemed to have what they wanted to try. In any case none of them knew Annie and they weren't even sure if it was true.

Once he did get involved in a fight, which started when the remarks became really dirty. Johnny had been brought up to respect women and old people and beneath his banter this was something he did. Although smaller than the other boy, Johnny was nimble and after jigging around him and not landing any punches for several minutes he ducked smartly beneath a below-the-belt one that he saw coming, with the result that the other boy shot forward on to the ground. There were cheers and jeers as he scrambled to his feet, and mopped a bleeding lower lip with a rather grubby handkerchief.

The school bell clanged then and an almost unscathed Johnny was slapped heartily on the back as they made their way inside the school.

The war was nearly four years old and he knew he would have to wait another three or four before he could officially get into the fray, if it lasted that long. The allies were making headway in North Africa and every night the entire family were quiet to listen to the news and wonder about Jim and Ron.

There had been more bombing in London during the early months of the the year but not on the scale of the blitz. One of the casualties in January was a junior school in Catford where he learned that two of their cousins had been killed.

'Poor Jill,' Mrs Bookman said, rubbing at her already red-rimmed eyes, 'and their father over there somewhere fighting for peace. It don't bear thinking about.'

She came into Johnny's room when he was getting ready for bed that night.

'Here's yer clean socks fer tomorrer, son,' she said, then leaned over and kissed him – something she had stopped doing at his request when he was about seven. Remembering his aunt and cousins, he didn't brush her away.

Easter wasn't until almost the end of April that year and Johnny became impatient to earn some real money. He left school and went to work in the same factory as his mother.

'But she's making bits for planes and I'm sweeping up the store,' he told Annie with a wry grin. He gave half his wages to his mother and spent the rest taking Annie out. Mrs Bookman continued to buy his clothes and the situation suited him well.

Annie too left school at Easter, and obtained a job in Bushton, serving in a music shop. She discussed the matter of staying on with the Dovers and paying for her lodgings rather than trying to find herself a place in Bushton. She knew that could prove difficult and she also reasoned that her parents would probably allow her to remain at a place they knew and approved of. Mrs Dover had grown fond of the girl and even her husband agreed that Anita Evesham on her own was no bother.

Her mother, however, did not approve of her prospective job.

'A shop assistant,' she said huffily, on the phone.

'In a first-class musical establishment,' Annie said, 'where I have the opportunity to meet some of the world's best musicians.'

Mrs Evesham, although she never suggested her daughter come home, tried to prevent her from working there, but Annie called her bluff.

'What alternative are you offering, Mummy?' she asked.

'Further education, of course. Especially in the social graces.'

'No.' Annie was unexpectedly firm. 'I can officially leave school and I intend to. If you can suggest a post for me in London I'll think about that, but I won't consider finishing-school. I want to work now until I'm old enough to join the Wrens.'

That was a second shock for her mother. 'The war will be over before that time comes, but if it isn't, and it is a very big if, Anita, then we shall see about getting you a high-ranking position.'

Annie laughed. 'I shall start at the bottom and work my way up. I don't want privileges. Life's more fun without them.'

She won her point and contined to live with the Dovers, offering them two shillings more than they had been receiving from the government. Her weekly allowance stayed the same as before and it was lack of coupons rather than money that prevented her from buying more than a couple of blouses and a nice black skirt for work. Mrs Dover's offer to make her a going out dress with material bought in Bushton market was welcomed. They also bought some curtain-net which was not on coupons to make a lacy blouse.

'I'll pay you back for doing this, of course,' Anita said, but Mrs Dover would not accept anything.

'I enjoy a bit of sewing, used to make most of Alison's clothes when she was a girl and the sewing machine needs to earn its keep.'

Annie travelled to Bushton each day on the train, mostly because she was accustomed to it and she didn't want the bother of finding lodgings in Bushton. More so because she didn't know how long she would stay in her job. She thought of it as a stepping-stone. She enjoyed what she did, and could converse well with the customers whether they were buying a piano or a mouth-organ. If it was a piano old Mr Jones the manager, used to hover and eventually take over.

It was great having the sheet-music to look at, too. Annie could play the piano passably, but as the Dovers did not possess an instrument she hadn't had an opportunity since 1939. Johnny had never learnt, 'but it'll be handy that you can play when we have a party,' he told her. 'That's if we can run to a joanna after we're married, gal.'

They still only met once a week, on a Sunday now, because both of them were working on Saturdays. One Sunday Johnny said, 'Thought we could go to my home for a meal today. Mum's looking forward to seeing you again.'

The visit was pleasant and she didn't have time to feel nervous about it. Mrs B was exactly as she remembered her from the time of Johnny's twelfth birthday, and after their meal she and Johnny walked in Victoria Park and he talked about when he was a little boy and played football where the barrage balloons were now anchored, and as a special treat, went to the zoo there. All too soon it seemed it was time for Annie to return to Winchurch. They went again a couple of times during the next few months, but only for a quick visit and a cup of tea because they were in the area. She found his dad hard to understand, although he made her welcome, but she warmed to his hard-working mum.

She continued her weekly letter to her parents, and occasionally telephoned them now that she was earning, but she had never suggested taking Johnny to her house, and he was very glad about that.

Twice a week Annie attended night-school in Bushton to learn shorthand and typing. Just before Christmas she found a suitable job in a publisher's office in London.

'I'll only be making the tea and doing the post at first,' she told Johnny. 'My shorthand is almost non-existent and my typing isn't up to the standard they would need yet, but I'll work on it. The important thing is that I'll be in London.'

She did not want to return home to live – she was adamant about that. For all these years now she had fended for herself in all but the practicalities of life. Both at the boarding-school and later in Winchurch. She did not think she could cope with life with her parents now, without a lot of stress for them all. There would be arguments, and, more important, she knew she would be greatly curtailed in her social arrangements.

Although they never said it in so many words, Annie knew her parents didn't want her at home either. It would disrupt their lives, especially her mother's, she thought. She had been away so long, and since her evacuation to the country she had not even returned for school holidays, as she had done before the war.

She and Johnny discussed where she would live. He wanted to ask his mother if Annie could lodge with them, but she hesitated. 'You haven't much room, anyway,

Johnny, and I wouldn't want you sleeping on that bedchair permanently, it wouldn't be right. Then there's the fares to think about. It will be much better if I find something near to my job. A hostel or something not too expensive to start with. I thought about trying for a job in a department store because I understand that some of them have their own hostels for their girls, but I doubt my parents would allow that. An office job though, that would be acceptable, I think.'

Although she didn't say so to him, Annie also wondered if she could live in such a poky house as his. She loved it on the few occasions she had visited for the day. There was a friendly warmth that was missing in her own background, but to live there all the time might not work out. Annie Evesham, you are what Johnny would call a bloody snob, she thought, and laughed to herself.

She secured the job and, by adding a couple of years to her age, a place at a small hostel, before she told her parents about it. It was touch and go for her because her mother came down to Winchurch the day she received Annie's letter with this news. Thank heaven she had sent it the beginning of a week she thought, because if it had arrived on a Saturday and Mrs Evesham had travelled to Kerry Avenue then and stayed the night it would have thrown her Sunday arrangements with Johnny out. And with no way of getting in touch with him it could have been chaotic. He might even have turned up at Kerry Avenue. Of course, it would have been even worse had she come on a Sunday, Annie thought, because she would either have been in, or on her way to, London to meet Johnny. As it was she got home from work in Bushton to find her mother drinking tea with Mrs Dover.

'I shall be staying at The Shepherd's Rest for the night,' Mrs Evesham informed her daughter, 'while we sort this mess out.'

Annie went along to the inn with her after dinner. She sat on the bed facing her mother who was in the only chair the room boasted.

'We sent you here to keep you safe,'Mrs Evesham said, 'and this is how you repay us. You're a wicked, deceitful girl, and you can write and cancel this job you say you have. I reluctantly agreed to you working in Bushton but you certainly are not returning to London.'

Annie was close to tears, but she took a deep breath and said in a quiet voice, 'I can't do that, I have given in my notice here and made plans to start the new job next Monday. It's all arranged.'

'Then unarrange it.'

The battle took over an hour, finishing with Annie sobbing into her already soaked handkerchief and Mrs Evesham still sitting impassively straight-backed and dry-eyed in the chair.

Annie stood up. 'I'd best get back,' she said.

'Yes, and I want to hear no more of this nonsense. When the war is over we shall all take a holiday and decide on your future. Meanwhile be thankful you have a comfortable safe place to stay, and parents who have your best interests at heart, and learn to be more grateful for it.'

As Annie walked back to Kerry Avenue the tears spilled down her cheeks and she brushed them away impatiently. She can't stop me, she thought, I shall be earning, I have somewhere to live, and although I suppose that in law she could force me to do as she wants, it would probably mean going to court and her pride would not let her do that because of what the neighbours might say.

She was glad she had not told her where she was working, nor where the hostel was. She knew she had been fortunate to get in but at her interview she had told them her parents lived too far away for her to live with them and nobody had questioned or checked on this statement.

She knew her mother hadn't asked for further details because in her mind the matter was settled. Annie would stay in Winchurch, work in Bushton and lodge with Mr and Mrs Dover until the war was over and her parents took up the reins again. Annie was sure the thought that her daughter would defy her to this extent had not entered her mother's mind.

She gave an enormous sniff as she turned into the Dovers' front gate. Her handkerchief was too saturated to use, and the tension of these last few hours slowly began to lift. Today was Thursday and on Monday she was booked into the hostel and also to begin her new job. No time for her parents to delve too much now that this evening was over, and she would telephone or write to them when she had been settled in for a few days.

For the first time in many years Annie was actually grateful that her mother had so little real interest in her movements that she had not asked more questions about which firm she was going to. With startling clarity she knew that Johnny's mum would have done so.

CHAPTER 11

1943

London was stimulating. Annie had a room to herself in the hostel. It was small, very small, but it was hers. Better than a dormitory, she thought, which was fine at boarding-school when you were younger, but since her time at Winchurch she had become used to her privacy.

'No boys in your room and indoors by ten o'clock unless you have special permission,' the warden said.

'Later, when I'm earning more money I expect I'll move into something more comfortable and with less restrictions,' she told Johnny.

They met several nights a week and went to the theatre or pictures, or simply walked the streets hand-in-hand and talked. Always there was something to talk about, some subject to probe and explore, a dream to visualize together. Annie was content.

Johnny was happy, and sometimes Annie's nearness

roused him to ecstatic heights and he'd push her from him when they were saying good-night.

The first time they made love was after a visit to the Piccadilly Theatre to see *Panama Hattie*. They walked back to the hostel and Annie said softly, 'Wouldn't it be marvellous if you didn't have to go home, Johnny? If you lived here too?'

'It's an all-girls hostel,' he said.

Annie laughed. 'I know, silly. I'm only dreaming. Just suppose you could get in. I'd make you a cup of coffee and we'd sit and drink it, and talk, and kiss good-night in warmth and comfort instead of in a murky old doorway where anyone can disturb us.'

'Don't Annie, don't,' he whispered agonizedly. 'Do you think I don't want to – oh Annie, Annie.' He held her close and his kisses were suddenly a man's and not a boy's.

'Listen, Johnny, I could sneak you in. Some of the girls do. And someone was going to open the window for me tonight because I hate asking for late-night passes.

'You *do* want to, Annie?' His eyes tried to probe the darkness and see her expression.

'Yes Johnny. Just as much as you, my love.'

The window at the back was on the catch as her friend had promised it would be. 'I'll do it as soon as the warden has been round,' she'd said, 'but don't make a noise getting through because she'll know it had to be one of us and I'm the most likely culprit.'

They went round the back of the building and Annie gently pushed the sash-corded window upwards sufficiently for her to climb in. Swiftly she looked along the corridor. All was quiet. With finger to her lips she beckoned to Johnny, and seconds later he was standing beside her. The window squeaked a little as they closed it, and Annie took hold of his hand and led him upstairs to her little room which was furnished with a chair, a chest of drawers, a small wardrobe and a bed.

He left half an hour later by the same window, which Annie secured with its brass bolt afterwards. She met no one as, barefooted and in her dressing-gown, she fled back upstairs. Bouncing on to her bed she laid on her back with her arms wrapped across her breasts and her eyes closed.

Johnny was waiting outside her office when she left work the following evening. His dark eyes searched her face tenderly.

'Are you all right, Annie?' he asked softly as she came up to him.

'Why yes.'

'I didn't hurt you?'

'No Johnny.'

He held both her hands. 'I do love you Annie,' he said.

Buses screeched to a halt at the stop outside her office; people jostled by on the pavement while they stood there together, oblivious to everything except their feelings for each other.

After that Annie knew she must find somewhere to live where she and Johnny could be together sometimes. Johnny still wanted her to lodge with them, but now more than ever Annie was against the idea.

'I couldn't look your mum in the face if I was living there, Johnny. I know that probably sounds silly to you,' she went on as he looked surprised, 'but she wouldn't like it, and we'd be forever on the jump.'

'She wouldn't know.'

'That's why I couldn't do it.'

The second time Johnny climbed in through the hostel window the sash-cord broke and he just missed having his neck severed. He was actually through when it came crashing down before he had time to turn round to close it.

'Quick,' Annie said, and they both raced upstairs to her room, until they could hear no more sounds downstairs. Then, with Annie's old coat and hood on as a flimsy disguise, he waited at the bend in the stairs while Annie knocked up the warden to say she felt ill. Peering over the banisters he saw her clutch the doorjamb and almost fall in. That was his cue to get away. There were two windows on the ground floor at the back, the broken sash-cord one and another that was identical and it was this second one, which was nearest to the warden's flat, that he had to unlock and escape through, while Annie kept the warden inside.

Of course he had missed the last bus home now, so he set off to walk, hoping his mother and father weren't out roaming the streets for him. He had told them he'd be late, so if luck was with him they would be asleep and would not realize what time he eventually arrived.

He was almost home when he heard planes overhead. Not the sound of British ones but the deeper noise and rhythm of the *Luftwaffe*. He hadn't heard the siren and thought it might have gone before he reached the area. In that case his mum would almost certainly be awake, so absolute quiet was called for. No noise or fumbling by the door. With this in mind he felt in his trouser-pocket for his key as he hurried along. It wasn't there. The planes had gone over now, leaving the echo of the throb of their engines in his whole body. Frantically he searched the other pocket, then the first one again. It had definitely gone. Must have fallen out when he climbed either in or out of one of the hostel windows tonight. At least they couldn't identify him from a key. It would only prove that someone had been in. And they wouldn't be able to connect that with Annie either, because there were at least six rooms on that floor. It did however, leave him with the problem of entering his own house. Well, there was nothing for it but to admit he'd lost his key. Wearily now he walked on. Better get into the vicinity, then he could say with truth that when he discovered he had lost it, he thought it was too late to knock them up. He needn't say just how late.

Johnny hurried down the narrow alley to the back gate, leant over it, and as silently as he could manage he unlatched it and went inside. The yard offered no comfort but with luck the shed wouldn't be locked. It seldom was. Carefully he tried it and the door opened. Johnny lay down on the floor, grateful to be back, and went fast asleep.

He woke early, conscious only of hearing planes overhead again during what was left of the night. He stretched himself a few times, then took off Annie's coat. It had certainly kept him warm in the night, but now was the time for planning. His mother would know it wasn't his, so it must be hidden. Looking around, he saw a bucket in the corner and stuffed the coat inside. Hope I remember to grab it and take it indoors later on, he thought.

All set now to explain his absence by the lost key, he suddenly had the most incredible slice of luck. The back kitchen door opened and his mother shook a cloth or duster or something, he couldn't make out what. As she was going back someone yoo-hooed from the side of the house, and she went down the narrow path connecting back and front to see who it was.

Johnny took full advantage. He pulled the coat from the bucket and dashed in through the still open back door, up the stairs and into his bedroom. As he leaned against the door he heard his mother's voice downstairs. It must be seven o'clock, and any minute now she would be up to make sure he was awake. He pulled back the bedcovers and rumpled them a bit, before hastily donning his pyjamas. Then he went to the bathroom to wash. Mrs Bookman was climbing the stairs. 'Goodness, Johnny, you startled me. I didn't hear you get up.'

Later, over breakfast she said, 'What time did you get in, Johnny? I was awake until after midnight listening.'

'Whatever for? I told you I wouldn't be early, Mum. We went to the pictures, then had a meal out.'

The lost key presented a problem, but he decided to say nothing until he was going out this evening. Then it would seem as though he'd lost it at work during the day.

At the bus-stop someone said, 'Bad do up the West End last night, then?'

'Where?'

'Trad Street. Early hours of the morning. Killed everyone

in the hostel there, and the blast damaged some of the others in the area too.'

Oh God. Annie. She was close to Trad Street.

When Johnny reached the area most of it was cordoned off. Men were working amongst the ruins of the Trad Street hostel. He spoke to the ARP warden there. 'The girls' hostel round the corner – were there any casualties there?'

'No one killed,' said the warden, 'not at any of the others. Blast damage, though, that's why you can't get round there. Who are you looking for?'

'Annie Evesham. She – she lives there.'

The warden consulted his list. 'She's not down here, son. They evacuated everyone from the houses and the girls' hostel afterwards, building not safe. Took 'em to St George's church hall, four – no five streets away. Try there.'

Johnny ran all the way. There was a woman in charge there, buxom, jolly-faced . . . but no Annie. 'What does she look like, son?'

'Bit taller than me, not much. Long dark-brown hair, very pretty.'

'Evesham.' She too looked at her list. 'Ah, here she is. She's gone to work. Left about half an hour ago. She your sister, son?'

Annie returned home to her parents after the hostel was damaged in what the papers began calling the little blitz.

'It's only temporary,' she told Johnny, 'but it's the best thing. Later I can say it's too far from my job and try for another hostel, but it isn't easy. I was lucky to get into that one. And even if I do manage to find a place I doubt if it will be a room on my own. So many of them are just dormitories. Maybe Mummy and Daddy will help with the rent of a small flat later on.'

'What, on your own, Annie?'

'Well no, they'll probably insist I share, but you see they don't want me home any more than I want to be there. You once said that you were 'an accident', Johnny. I hadn't thought about it before, but I think I really must have been too. They couldn't wait to push me off to boarding-school, and then later evacuation. I was lucky that it wasn't to America – Daddy stopped that. He likes to see me sometimes.'

'Will I still be able to see you, Annie?'

'Of course you will, silly. But we'll have to be careful. You know, with me being watched all the time. But don't worry, Johnny, I'll think of something, and with spring and summer coming it should be easier.'

It was. Annie invented a friend with whom she worked. Rosanna, she called her, because one of her favourite songs at that time was Rosanna, *My Lovely Russian Rose*. Rosanna had more freedom than anyone Mrs Evesham knew.

'Well, she is a year older than me,' Annie explained, 'and she loves classical music so much. You can't leave before the end of a concert, but if I had a door-key it wouldn't disturb you both if I came in late after a concert or show.' For Rosanna also liked to keep up with the latest shows on in town.

It wasn't easy. Mr Evesham came up with the suggestion that she might like to bring Rosanna home with her one weekend, but, she was sure to her mother's great relief,

Annie found many reasons why it was impractical.

Rosanna had an invalid mother whom she helped to look after, so she couldn't stay away overnight. Her invalid mother also happened to be a widow, which meant she relied totally on Rosanna's support.

The fuss over giving her a key highlighted again the differences between her and Johnny's life styles. Johnny had a key so that he could let himself in should his mother be out any time.

Annie's father came to the rescue, saying what a good idea it was. 'Of course she can't leave before the end, Eunice,' he said. 'It makes sense for her to have a key. Anita is a sensible girl and not likely to hand it over to a burglar, after all.'

Smiling at his wife now he added, 'I seem to remember you were given a key when we were engaged because your parents went to bed early.'

Annie held her breath. Dear Dad, he didn't know how close to the truth he was, she thought. The reference to those days seem to have a softening effect on his wife, however, and after a moment or two of silence she said, 'I suppose it wouldn't hurt. I do deplore the manners of those people who rush out before the national anthem is played.'

Turning to her daughter she said, 'All right, you may have a key but it isn't a licence to be late every evening. Only when you go to a late-night concert. Otherwise we expect you to leave your friend's house and be back here at a reasonable time.'

Rosanna could not, however, solve the problem of where

Annie and Johnny could go to do their courting. Strolling hand in hand through the streets of London they were well content, and as the evenings grew warmer they found secluded spots beneath the trees.

Jim and Ron, although brothers, had not 'claimed' each other, the Bookmans explained to Annie.

'It's a thing they *could* do, the older one 'claiming' the younger one to serve in his unit so they would be together, sort of looking after each other, but we're glad they decided against it. Too dodgy,' Charlie Bookman said. 'Best to be in different regiments, fighting different battles, they both stand a chance then, we reckoned, didn't we, duck?' He looked across to his wife and they gave each other the sort of intimate smile Annie had come to recognize as a signal of their love for each other.

When Italy surrendered in September 1943 Charlie said with fervour, 'Winnie's right, we're well on the way.'

Annie, looking towards Maggie Bookman, saw her press her hands together as though in prayer, and kept back the words she had been going to say.

CHAPTER 12

1944

Everywhere they went in the spring of 1944, Johnny and Annie saw signs of something big stirring. London was full of troops of every nationality. One of Ron's closest friends, whose parents lived along the street from the Bookmans, was killed at the battle of Cassino.

On their evening walks throughout May they encountered army vehicles rumbling through the streets and out of London. All the talk was of the second front, the invasion of France and on the 8 o'clock news on the 6 June, the first reports of the landings came over. An hour and a half later these were officially confirmed when John Snagge announced, 'D-Day has come. Early this morning the allies began the assault on the north-western face of Hitler's European fortress.' The following morning the headlines in all the papers said D-Day. *Allies land in France.*

'Reckon it really will be all over by Christmas now,

Annie. I'll get me barrow yet,' Johnny said a few days later. 'I'm glad I'm not a man,' said Annie. 'I used to think I'd like to be at one time. Men can do so much more than women. Well, they could before the war, but now women are coming into their own, so watch out, Johnny.'

He laughed. 'I'm glad you're not a man, Annie.'

'It must be terrifying to be amongst those first ones who landed in France,' she said.

'Exciting too. We're the conquering ones now. Don't think I realized before how awful it would have been if we'd been invaded, Annie. Somehow I couldn't imagine it.'

It was a wonderful summer for them, and Annie had plans to move into Rosanna's family's spare bedroom by the autumn, if she could persuade her parents of the advantages. She reeled them off to Johnny one evening. 'Nearer my work, I can give a hand with Rosanna's mother, cheaper, and safer,' she giggled, 'than living on my own. And my trump card, Johnny, I know they want to go to America to see my aunt, Mummy's sister, and now that I'm working I can't go with them. And I would hate to stay in the house all alone . . .'

Johnny laughed and hugged her. 'I hope you won't manipulate me like this when we're married, Annie.'

She looked suitably shocked. 'Of course not. I'm doing this for you.'

Johnny's mum often packed sandwiches for them during those summer Sundays.

'Do be careful,' she would say as they set off.

Frequently they took the Green Line bus into the country, and with their haversack rations walked, talked and loved each other.

Once Mrs Bookman said tentatively, 'Johnny, you and Annie are still children, really you know. Fifteen might seem grown-up to you but growing up isn't just what age you are. Don't you think you ought to mix with other friends more? What do her parents think about you two always going off together?'

'Her parents don't care a jot about her, Mum,' Johnny replied, 'and don't worry because I wouldn't hurt Annie for all the gold in the world.'

They had a wonderful summer. Mr and Mrs Evesham did not go to America after all. 'We shall wait until the war is over now it's heading that way, then we will know you are safe,' was the reason Mrs Evesham gave to Annie.

Annie smiled to herself over this. Perhaps it salved their consciences, she thought, the fact that they were doing everything possible to make her *safe*. Safe from what? From the bombs? Well, no one was completely safe from them, wherever they lived, although some areas were of course safer than others, she conceded.

She realized that they thought she was safe from boys too, now that she was living at home. Most of her own age-group seemed like children to her, but the city was full of troops passing through on leave. Many of them were a long way from their own homes and were very lonely. Some girls her age were boy-mad, she knew, but from the moment she saw him she had only wanted Johnny. She didn't know what the attraction was, and at first she hadn't wanted or needed him in a loving sense. But the magnetism was there right from the start, when she saw him following Mrs Dover up the stairs, a tiny, frightened but defiant child.

Perhaps that was what she loved about him, his fierce independent spirit – or was it those huge dark eyes in that high-cheek-boned pale face? Or the way he made her laugh? She hadn't known then and she didn't now. It wasn't love she thought, not right at the beginning, but the seeds were sown then and they grew alarmingly. Sometimes it frightened her how much she loved him.

She looked at flats nearer to her work, but as well as being scarce they were pricey and she wasn't earning the sort of money to keep up with those rents. Sharing would be the answer, but she didn't fancy sharing with anyone, except Johnny, she giggled to herself. If the chance to share but still have your own room occurred, she would consider it, but meanwhile the best way to save was to live at home. Her father gave her a dress-allowance, and as clothes were on coupons some of this she saved.

She hadn't talked to Johnny about money yet, not in a serious way. She knew he didn't earn as much as she did, but that didn't matter. It would be their joint income that would count when they were wed. Five years seemed long enough to put a bit in the bank now that they were both working, but Annie knew that Johnny actually kept very little of his wages. After he had given his mother some, she was sure the rest went on their outings. He would seldom allow her to open her purse.

They hadn't discussed where they would live when they were married either, but she had her own ideas about this.

Somewhere in the country perhaps. It would have to be a small place at first, but she didn't mind that. Not Winchurch or Bushton, they were too far from London, but there were many places she had passed through on the train in the days when she was travelling up to meet Johnny every Saturday. One of those would do nicely. Johnny had enjoyed the countryside once he had settled down and they could rent a little shop and work it up together.

The doodlebugs, which gave an eerie warning as they cut out, and later, in September the V2s, rockets which gave no warning and left a huge crater, were still coming over, but Annie pushed the idea that either of them might not survive to the very back of her mind. Our troops were getting closer to Germany every week, and optimism in the country was high.

In the autumn Annie had promotion; she went to the inner office to work and a new girl came to do the post, run the errands and make the tea. Her new position carried with it a rise in pay. 'Not a lot,' she told Johnny, 'but it will add to our savings.'

'What savings, Annie?'

'For later when we get married.'

'Blimey, Annie, it'll be years and years yet.'

'I know that,' she answered placidly, 'but if I start now we'll have something in the bank when we need it, Johnny.'

'But I'm not contributing. That's your money and it isn't fair for you to go without things.'

'I've got everything I want, Johnny, honestly.'

He was silent for so long she thought she had really upset him, then he said suddenly, ' 'Course, when we are married, Annie, I'll have my own barrow. I'll make a bit more then.'

'Later you might be able to have a shop, Johnny, have you thought about that?'

'Not really, but I suppose we could. Be warmer than the barrow in the winter. Depends when the war's over though, doesn't it, gal, and how much the rents are? You've more overheads with a shop.'

She left the thought with him and snuggled close. 'There's plenty of time,' she said.

By Christmas victory looked certain, but when? On the wireless Adelaide Hall was singing 'The Happiest New Year Of All', and Annie saw Mrs Bookman wipe the tears from her eyes when she heard the song. There were photographs of Jim and Ron in their army uniform, standing either side of the mantelpiece, and when she was there one Saturday night, waiting for Johnny and his dad to come home, Mrs Bookman picked them up and said, 'One thing, Annie, the war should be over now before Johnny has a chance to join up.'

'Yes. You'll be glad to see your other sons home, too.'

'It's not finished yet,' Mrs Bookman said cautiously, 'and there's a lot gone. Young men, and women, who had all their living to do. It's a wicked world, Annie.'

Johnny and his dad came in then, and the quiet moments were broken, but Annie felt that Mrs Bookman had at last accepted her as part of the family. She thought, she realizes that Johnny and I will get married one day, and she was talking to me woman to woman.

Annie spent Christmas Day with the Bookmans, although her parents thought she was spending it with Rosanna and her mother. But on Boxing Day she stayed in with her own parents. She didn't invite Johnny because she knew he would hate it, and she wasn't sure whether her mother would agree anyway. If she didn't, Annie thought, we would quarrel, and it would do no good.

She had passed her first typing examination in the autumn and now with a working knowledge of book-keeping, sixty words a minute on the typewriter, and a basic knowledge of shorthand – her speed wasn't too good yet but she was working on that – she had hopes of find-ing a more lucrative paying job in the New Year.

CHAPTER 13

In December 1944 there was heavy fighting in the hills and forests of the Ardennes in Eastern Belgium. The fog and wintry weather, and the difficult terrain, kept the battle raging for six weeks.

Annie and Johnny knew the Bookmans were worried because there had been no word from Ron. There was a brief note from Jim in time for Christmas, on which he had drawn a rotund and cheeky-looking snowman. Charlie Bookman tried to jolly them all along by saying how unreliable the post could be at times like this and, with all the greetings coming and going, his was probably in a bag that had got pushed to the bottom of the pile or even sunk at sea.

As January blew the icy winds across the channel to Britain even he refrained from comment, at least within Johnny's and Annie's hearing.

It was the beginning of February 1945 when Ron was reported 'missing, believed killed.' Mrs Bookman took the news as Annie would have expected, with great courage.

Johnny was inconsolable.

He swore and shouted, cursed and cried, but only with Annie. 'I have to keep up the pretence that he isn't dead when Mum's around,' he said, one night. 'She's clinging to that "believed killed" bit. Not proven. But Annie, he's dead, otherwise they'd know where he was.'

'I think you're right, Johnny, but, although your mum's hoping and praying for Ronnie's return, I think she realizes and accepts this too. But, well, it's that streak of optimism in her, Johnny. I think she's been marvellous.'

'And I haven't?'

'I didn't say that.'

It was their first quarrel, and it took off in a way that scared them both. And although in the end they weren't arguing over the implied criticism, but over deeper issues of their ability to understand the other's feelings, it hurt Annie badly that such a tragedy could start it up. They stood at the bus-stop in silence. Never before had the bus seemed to take such a time. It usually arrived much too quickly for them. Annie broke the strain. 'Don't wait,' she said, 'I can manage.'

Johnny walked off. Seconds before the bus arrived he returned, seeming to materialize by her side in the queue without her seeing him coming. 'Sorry, Annie. I'm a bit het up,' he said.

Her eyes filled with tears. 'I'm sorry too, Johnny. I didn't mean any of the bad things I said.'

'Nor me. Blast, here's the bus. Tomorrow night?'

'I'll come round straight from work.'

They didn't stay in. Mrs Bookman urged them out,

Annie suspected that it was so she need not put on a brave face any longer.

It was too cold for walking for long, yet neither were in the mood for the pictures, so they went to the Express Dairies, their favourite drinking place. They sat on high stools and talked about Ron. 'Jim'll take it hard,' Johnny said. 'They were close. Being so much younger I was never part of their set-up, but I – well, I guess I looked up to them both in my way. Yes, they were both my heroes. I feel so mean, Annie, I grumbled because Mum left Ron's stuff in the bedroom when I came home. I wanted to clear it all out. Now, well, I don't know what to do. I lay in bed last night and looked up at his shelf and I – I blubbed like a baby, Annie.'

'Johnny, oh Johnny, I wish I could help, but there's nothing I can say that would, is there? It is *just* possible that he's a prisoner, or injured, but—'

'I know. I hope, well I just hope it was quick, Annie. See, that's one of the things about it: we don't know. Either where he is or where he died, or how. I don't know why, but it would help I think, if we knew.'

They bought another hot chocolate and spun it out, then they walked very slowly towards the bus-stop. Johnny wanted to take Annie right home, but she insisted that he simply waited with her until the bus came each time.

'Where is the sense in you coming all that way and then having to come back again, probably walk back too if we were very late? The bus stops almost outside our place anyway, so I have hardly any distance to travel.'

'I always time it, Annie,' he said. 'Those eerie doodlebugs are still coming over. And the V2s. It's not over yet.'

'It's like your mum says, Johnny, "If it's got your name on you'll cop it, and if it hasn't you'll be one of the miraculous escapes we read about".'

The bus hove in to sight, lumbering along from the gloom of the night. 'I love you, Annie,' he said as he gave her a quick kiss before she boarded.

Annie didn't tell her parents about Ron because she had never told them about Johnny. She thought her mother was much too naïve to believe that she had stopped seeing him when she was told to. But if she believed it then it served her purpose for the myth to continue. Annie suspected that her mother, while wanting to do her duty as a parent, would rather have had no children. They had never been close because they had never been together. From the age of seven Annie had been away at school, even sometimes during the holidays if her parents had been in America visiting her mother's sister.

That argument didn't always hold good with her because she knew girls at boarding-school who were close to their parents. It depends on the reason they send you, she thought. Our children, Johnny's and mine, will not be sent away to school until they are old enough to cope with the separation. A good education yes, but a home too. Like Johnny's home, but wealthier. Or was she being a snob again?

Four and a half weeks later, in early March, news of Ron's safety arrived. The family joy was tempered with sorrow that he was minus a leg.

'But that's nothing,' Mrs Bookman was quick to point out, 'in return for his life.'

Doris, Jim's wife who had come round that evening to hear about it said, 'I hope he thinks so.'

'They'll fit him with a wooden one eventually, and there won't be much he'll miss out on, Doris. Look at Douglas Bader – both his legs gone yet he leads the same sort of life as if he still had them.'

'Maybe he's the exception.'

'Aw, don't be a Jeremiah, Doris. Ron's alive and that's all that matters. To him as well as us. I'm sure of it.'

Annie was quiet. She could understand Doris's point of view, but she knew also that if it was Johnny they would cope. And Ron hadn't left a regular girlfriend behind as far as she knew, so any girl who took him on would know the score right from the beginning.

Ron was flown home later in the month and Annie went with Johnny and his parents to the Cambridge Military Hospital in Aldershot to see him.

'Lost me tag in the bloody battle, and I'm not swearing. That's what it was,' he told them. 'That's why they said I was missing. They didn't know who I was 'til I was patched up a bit an' in a fit state to talk to 'em. Lost me bloody leg, not me memory or me marbles, I said to the doc and he laughed. He was a blooming hero, that man. Worked night and day 'e did.'

Ron was cheerful and looking forward to coming home.

'Back in Blighty, that's all we've wanted these last years, most of us. And there's many worse off than me,' he told them. 'I felt bitter at first, but when you look around these places you see things different like. See, about the only thing I'm not going to be able to manage is a bike, and that won't worry me too much. I'd rather have a car anyway when I've got the ready. They said I would be able to drive a specially adapted car and I'd get help.'

'Hope they keep their word this time,' Charlie muttered in the background, 'I remember the last war and the promises.'

Annie and Ron had not met before and as they were leaving Ron said, 'Can I kiss your girlfriend, Johnny? You beat me to it young'un – now if I'd seen her first . . .' They all laughed as Annie leaned over the bed and kissed him.

It was a relieved family who boarded the train to take them back to London that day.

'He's got the right spirit,' Maggie Bookman said quietly. 'It mightn't be as easy as he says now, but he'll get by. Some of those poor blighters in there made yer heart bleed. At least our Ron's still got one good leg and both his 'ands and 'arms.'

Charlie took her hand in his. 'You're a happy woman now you've seen him, aren't you, duck?'

' 'Course I am. And don't tell me you weren't worried by how he'd be too, Charlie Bookman,'cos I wouldn't believe you.'

Johnny nudged Annie and they grinned at each other as the train steamed its way back to the capital.

The war in Europe was drawing to a close, the allies advancing steadily. Jim wrote home to say that even the Germans were hanging out welcome flags.

'You know, Annie,' Johnny said to her one evening,

'there's a bit of me that's disappointed. I know that's an awful thing to say, but I'd have liked to do my bit, and now that it's all going to be over by the summer I shan't get a chance.'

'Johnny Bookman, it's more than awful, it's a wicked, wicked thing to say or even think. Your mum was right the other week when she said it's the men who cause the wars. Look at you, spoiling for a fight, wanting to have a go. Surely you don't want to risk getting your legs shot off too?'

Johnny had seldom seen her so passionately angry. 'You don't understand, Annie. I suppose women look at these things differently. I'd hate leaving you and I reckon I'd be scared when it came to actual fighting, but I'd be there, a part of it.'

'Rubbish. War's not like a fisticuffs in the school playground, Johnny.'

'Anyway it won't happen, so that's that. It will all be over before my time comes, but I still feel a bit cheated.'

'Well, your mum and I feel relieved.'

Things were working reasonably well at the Evesham home.

Annie insisted on paying her mother a small amount each week now that she was living back with them. She left fairly early in the morning to get to work in Clerkenwell and always made sure to say whether she would be in for dinner in the evening or not. Her father asked her about her work and she told him the truth: that she was really a general dogsbody in the office at present.

'Even with promotion I'm only second from the lowliest

one there, but I don't mind that, I'm learning a lot about the book trade, and after the war, when there's more paper about, we shall take off, I'm sure. Might even write a book myself one day, you never know.'

Her mother maintained a hurt silence about it all and Annie never volunteered extra information in case it rebounded on her. She knew how disappointed her mother was that she had rejected plans for finishing-school and what she called 'a good marriage.'

When they decided the time was right now for them to make that visit to America, which they had been planning for so long, it was her mother who said, 'Could you go and live with Rosanna for six months while we're away, Anita? I think that is the best plan. You're there more often than at home anyway,' she added.

'Sure. When are you wanting to go?'

'End of the month. We shall return in October, so you can have Christmas at home.'

'I'll pop in from time to time and check on the place,' Annie said. 'You go and enjoy yourselves.'

'There will be no need to check.' Mrs Evesham looked at her daughter. 'We shall let the house while we're gone. That has been taken care of.'

Annie, who had had visions of living at home and saving the money she would have paid in rent was stunned.

'Letting it? Why? I mean I could just have wanted to stay on, you know.'

'I thought you couldn't wait to move in with Rosanna, and this arrangement suits us, Anita. Mr and Mrs Peckham

need a base for six months. They come highly recom-
mended. Even so, I shall put some of the expensive break-
ables away, but the rest of the furniture and fittings will
stay as they are. We would like to meet Rosanna and her
parents before we go, naturally.'

'Oh. Yes, of course. I'll arrange something,' Annie said,
wondering how she was going to get out of this one.

'You tell one lie, Johnny,' she said to him that evening,
'and it rebounds a hundred times. What do I say now? I
don't want to get in any deeper.'

'You'll have to live somewhere, Annie. Have you any
relatives or friends in London? Wish our house was bigger.
I know you didn't want to come to us, and now with Ron
coming home it wouldn't be possible, but it would be good
if you were living near.'

'That's an idea, Johnny. If I could find a place close to
you and your family . . .'

'I'll keep my ear to the ground,' said Johnny. 'Sure to be
something, but what you tell your parents I really don't
know.'

'I suppose I'll have to tell them another lie. Say that
Rosanna is leaving. Oh heck.'

When Mrs Bookman learned of the dilemma, without
the deceit of the invented Rosanna, of course, simply that
Annie needed lodgings for six months while her parents
were away, she said calmly, 'Don't rush it. You can stay
here while you're looking, dear. Ron won't be home for
some time yet and if Johnny doesn't mind sleeping downstairs on the bedchair, you can have his room.'

Annie demurred. Nothing would make her say that her

parents, if they came to see, would not entertain her living in the cosy little house that she had come to love. If only I were a few years older I could go my own way, she thought, but at present the law could probably make me conform.

She began a search for suitable accommodation immediately, looking, as Johnny had suggested, in his area. After all she was travelling a good distance to work now, which defeated her original argument anyway.

CHAPTER 14

Annie was at home the evening her father had a heart attack. It was a rare occasion, for normally she saw Johnny every night, either at his house or in town. But that evening she was working late and Johnny was going to the hospital to see his brother. 'I won't come round afterwards,' she said, 'I'll have a night indoors, wash my hair and everything, it will save doing it on Sunday morning.'

She had come out of the bathroom, the towel round her head Carmen Miranda fashion, when she heard this odd sort of strangled cry. Almost like a cat caught in something, but they had no pets. She stood at the top of the stairs and listened. There it was again. Puzzled she went downstairs to investigate, and found her father rolling in pain on the floor.

'Dad. Oh no.' She ran to him and he gasped, 'Doctor. Fetch . . .'

She ran into the hall and phoned 999, then rushed back to him. 'It's all right, there's an ambulance on the way. Is it easier?'

He actually tried to smile at her, but his face twisted into a grimace and although the sweat was running in rivulets down his cheeks he felt icy-cold.

Mrs Evesham was at a meeting, and she came in as the ambulance arrived. Only one of them was allowed to go with him, so Annie reluctantly stayed behind.

'Ring me from the hospital,' she pleaded with her mother, 'as soon as he's in bed, and tell me how he manages the journey, how he is.'

She went in and closed the heavy front door. It was nearly an hour later when Mrs Evesham telephoned. 'Your father has had a heart attack, Anita. I'm staying here the night.'

'Will he – is he – going to be all right?' There was silence for a few moments, then Mrs Evesham's voice again, thick with tears. 'We don't know, but if he can get through the night there's a chance.' And for the first time in her life Annie heard her mother crying.

The phone went dead while she was trying to think of something comforting to say. Afterwards she longed for Johnny, but because the Bookmans hadn't a telephone she couldn't contact him without being out of the house for hours, and she was afraid to do that, just in case. . . .

She phoned the hospital early the following morning and was told that her father had had a comfortable night. That was all. Just before she left the house the telephone rang and this time it was her mother, who said she was coming home for a few hours.

'I'm just off to work, Mummy, but I'll be home this evening. You – you can reach me at the office if – if you want me,' she added tremulously. 'I'll leave the number on the pad.'

It was an hour before her normal time, but she wanted to break her journey and see Johnny before going to work.

'I'll meet you and come to the hospital with you this evening,' he said when she told him the news.

If Mrs Evesham was surprised to see him, indeed if she even recognized him as the boy with her daughter at Buckingham Palace two years before, she gave no sign. Seemingly completely composed again now, she outlined the hospital instructions to her daughter.

Johnny went to the hospital with them but only immediate family were allowed in. He was in the waiting-room downstairs when Annie returned. 'I think he's going to be all right, Johnny. He is very ill, they said, but he looks better. It really frightened me how he looked the night it happened.'

'Well, we can spend the evening here and you can pop in and see him again.'

'No, Sister said no excitement and only one person there. Mummy is staying for a while then she'll go on home. I said we were going out but that I wouldn't be late in.'

'And she didn't try to stop you?'

'No. I think she's still in shock, Johnny. You know it's – it's really shaken her up.' They left the hospital hand in hand.

The American visit plans had to be cancelled, and also the renting of the house.

'Of course there is no need for you to go to Rosanna's now, Anita,' Mrs Evesham said later in the week.

'No, of course not, Mummy.' Johnny had not been back to the house with Annie, and she told him her mother hadn't mentioned him at all.

'Well, we'll see what happens,' he said, 'but it would be good if she accepted that we're courting, because whatever her attitude, it won't make any difference to us, Annie. You're for me, there'll never be another.'

When Annie missed a period she put it down to shock over her father's heart attack. A few days later she realized that her breasts felt exceptionally tender. Did that happen when you were pregnant? She didn't know, but the missed period now began to bother her. Surely she couldn't be pregnant? It must be the shock of her father's illness. It had affected her more deeply than she would have expected a few months ago.

When Johnny said one evening, 'Hey, dreamer, where are you? I've spoken to you three times without a flicker of response,' she flared back at him.

'All right, all right, keep your hair on. It wasn't important really, but it's nice to get an answer sometimes.' He reached out and smoothed her hair. 'I love you, Annie.' Annie burst into tears.

She sobbed on his shoulder for some time, yet she couldn't tell him what was wrong. Not until she was sure. And somewhere inside her she knew it couldn't be true – it hadn't happened before, and at first she had been afraid it might, so why now? No, it was coincidence. Worry and shock did halt periods she knew, she had read it somewhere and that must be what was happening. By next month she would be back on an even keel with everything.

'Sorry, Johnny.' She lifted her head. He took his hand-kerchief from his pocket and gently wiped her eyes.

'That's OK. I didn't mean to make you cry, darling. You're still pretty worried about your old man, aren't you? But he is going on all right, you know. The hospital would tell your mother otherwise.'

Ron was told he would be discharged within a couple of weeks, and the last letter they had received from Jim was optimistic and full of plans for when the war was over.

'You know, Annie,' Johnny said one evening over a snack meal before they went to the pictures, 'I've been thinking about your idea of a shop instead of a barrow. I don't want to be poor all me life. And Ron'll have to have something to give him a start – Dad's business won't support us all. Mum's earning good wages now in the factory, but she'll be out of a job when the war's over, and when you and I get married we'll need to be on our own anyway. So what do you think about me trying to get a job in a shop as a start, and looking around for a place to rent?'

'Sounds fine, Johnny. What sort of place? I mean, what would we sell?'

'Fruit and veg, I suppose. It's the only thing I know how to sell. I was helping me dad with that when I was a nipper. Buying too, from the market. See, I wouldn't know how much with anything else than coster stuff.'

'It sounds OK to me, Johnny. I'll help too, later, after we're married, but until we are I can keep on with my job. It's not a bad wage now. Unless of course I have to go when the men come back from the war. I don't know how

I stand with my firm.'

She was still worried as to whether she was pregnant, and wished she really did have a friend called Rosanna in whom she could confide. In books and articles she had read the mother-to-be always suffered from morning sickness, and Annie clung to the hope that it was a false alarm triggered by the trauma of her father's illness, because she definitely hadn't been or even felt the slightest bit sick in the mornings or any other time.

Her next period was almost due, and she banked all her hopes now on that.

CHAPTER 15

Johnny felt buoyant. Victory in Europe was imminent, and within a short while surely victory in Japan too. Ron was home and managing well on his crutches. He was looking forward to having the wooden leg fitted. 'Be as good as new then,' he boasted. He had turned the coster-barrow idea down quickly.

'I want to get into industry,' he said. 'Cars, that'll be the thing of the future. In ten years' time everyone who wants one will have a car and I aim to be in on this potential money maker.' He and his dad had several friendly arguments about it and Ron was adamant. 'It's going to be different from what it was like after the last war,' he said. 'We're all better educated, and after six years fighting we know what we want for our country. A Labour government for a start, a government for the working people.'

Annie half-listened to this talk when she was in Johnny's house, and pondered about it in the privacy of her bedroom at home. She had never taken notice of politics and government before, but now, with her and Johnny's previous life styles being so different from each other, she began to think about the kind of Britain she wanted for them both.

She was still worried in case she was expecting a baby, yet part of her refused to believe this could be so. Physically she felt fine. Each day she ran her hands across her stomach and it was as flat as before. The tenderness in her breasts persisted. In two days' time her period was due again. And she was sure that this time it would come. Beyond that she refused to think.

When it didn't she knew she had to do something about it. She did feel sick now, but it was the deep-welled sickness of desperation. Whatever would they do if she was with child?

She made an appointment with a doctor in London, picking his name from the telephone book in the office, and phoning from a call-box during her lunch-hour. The doctor, when she visited, was very gentle with her.

'How old are you and what makes you think you might be pregnant?' he asked.

'Sixteen,' she said tremulously, 'and, yes I could be. I have a regular boyfriend and . . .' close to tears now, and not knowing how to put the act into words her voice dropped to barely a whisper. 'We . . . I . . . we have loved each other.'

The doctor looked at her thoughtfully. 'I'll do some tests,' he said. She paid his receptionist and tried to put the matter from her mind but it was impossible. She had to wait a week for the results of the tests, and she didn't know how she was going to get through it. Unless by some miracle she came on before the week was up.

Her father was now on the mend, although still in hospital. 'No sudden shocks or stresses,' the heart specialist told them.

'Of course not,' Mrs Evesham said. 'We lead a very quiet sedate life, there will be nothing to bring on another attack. I expect it was the strain of the war.'

Annie wondered how that could be, but she supposed that even for her father and mother, who appeared to have carried on their lives in the same way apart from a few restrictions they could do nothing about, the war had taken its toll. She doubted if she could have told them about a baby in the normal way, but she knew now that, if it were true, telling them in the circumstances was impossible. So she began to make plans. But her brain didn't seem to be functioning fully any longer, and she only got as far as returning to Winchurch or Bushton, finding a job and some lodgings, and having her baby there, away from everyone she knew in London.

And Johnny, she would have to tell him and he would be the one to visit her then, as she had travelled to meet him every week when they were parted before. And as soon as they legally could they would marry. Unless, unless he rejected her then. Boys didn't marry girls who ... but Johnny would. It was his baby too. And somehow they would have to manage until that time. Annie cast her mind back to all the books she had read where a girl had a child out of wedlock.

She returned to see the doctor on 7 May, and had her worst suspicions confirmed. He advised her to see her own doctor and to tell her parents, which in the quiet of his room and with his concerned eyes upon her, she agreed to do.

She had to jostle her way through the crowds when she came from the surgery, for in spite of daylong speculation about a German surrender, and no official announcement, the people were celebrating anyway. There seemed to be thousands about, on the pavements, in the roads, some even climbing the lampposts!

Her pregnancy wasn't such a shock as she had thought it would be. Over the past few weeks, in spite of telling herself that it was not so, she had partly prepared herself for the news. She wasn't seeing Johnny until the following day, and she felt no desire to change the arrangement. It would give her time to plan her words. . . .

The knowledge that the tests were positive didn't truly hit her until she was on the way to Johnny's house the following evening. Winston Churchill had broadcast to the nation at three o'clock, and Victory in Europe was official. At nine the King was to be on the air. The war was over, and the peace had started. But she had to tell Johnny about the baby. Before she left she checked with her mother that she would be all right.

'Yes, thank you, Anita. I shall visit your father as usual, then come home and listen to the happy news on the wireless.'

She didn't even remonstrate with her to 'be careful', Annie went with a heavy heart now to meet Johnny.

The family had been joined by Jim's wife, Doris, her parents, and several neighbours, and the rejoicing was in full swing when Annie arrived. Everyone there kissed her, someone gave her a Union Jack and Johnny put his arm round her shoulder and said, 'We're all going up to Trafalgar Square, that all right with you, Annie?'

'I . . . yes . . . I suppose so.'

He squeezed her shoulder. 'It's going to be a night we'll always remember,' he said.

At one point during the dancing Annie thought, maybe I shall lose the baby doing this, isn't that what happens sometimes? Maybe I won't need to tell Johnny at all.

She seemed to be standing outside herself, conscious of the dancers and the singing, the jubilation and cap-over-the-windmill atmosphere; yet a small core held back and wrestled still with the shattering knowledge that she was expecting a baby, and she had to tell Johnny.

At ten minutes to twelve she could suddenly stand it no longer. 'Johnny.' She plucked at his sleeve. 'Johnny, can we go somewhere quiet? I have to talk to you.'

Amazed, he looked at her. 'You've got to be joking, gal, where would you find somewhere quiet on a night like this?'

'I don't know Johnny, but we must. It's terribly impor-tant.'

'All right. Keep close to me and we'll try to find our way out of this crowd.' Holding hands they wove in and out of the celebrators, several times getting caught up again in the exuberant dancing.

'Come on, youngsters, tag on the end,' an elderly man wearing a paper hat said, and he put his arm round Annie's waist in an effort to get them to join his line of high-kicking, dancing people.

In a shop doorway, away from the concentrated crowds, Johnny took her in his arms and kissed her passionately. Some sailors going past called out cheerily. Annie pushed him away. 'I want to talk, Johnny.'

'What is it, Annie? You've gone as white as a sheet. Aren't you well?'

'I saw the doctor yesterday, Johnny, and I'm going to have a baby.'

At first he didn't seem to understand. 'You're going to have a baby?' he repeated.

When she didn't answer he said again, 'A baby?'

She nodded, for suddenly no further words would come.

'But . . . oh Annie. When?'

'In the . . . in the autumn. The doctor thought about November. Oh, Johnny, what are we going to do? I can't, I can't tell my people, it would kill Dad now.'

'We'll get married,' he said. 'Yes, we'll be married sooner than we thought, that's all.'

'Will they let us, Johnny? How old do you have to be?'

'I don't know, Annie, but Mum'll know. She'll know what to do about the baby too. Oh Annie, does it hurt?'

She was crying as she said, 'Of course it doesn't, not yet anyway. Johnny, you do want to marry me, don't you? I mean, you don't have to, you know. I . . . I could go away somewhere and have the baby quietly. I've got some money saved, then it could, could be adopted . . .'

That seemed to jolt Johnny out of his stupor.

'Never. It's our kid. Maybe we're a bit young to be

parents, Annie, but we'll manage. I'll get a job, a better job, and we'll find some rooms somewhere. Look, let's . . let's go home now.' He looked at his watch. 'The others won't be in for ages – even Ron's gone round to a pal's house for the night, and we can sort ourselves out, like.' Gently he put his arm round her again and kissed her, 'Why, you're shivering Annie. Are you cold? Come on, we'll get home and have a nice cup of tea.'

They telephoned Mrs Evesham from the first box they came to, to find out how Annie's father was and to tell her that Annie was staying the night with Johnny's family. Then, while the rest of them were singing and dancing the hours away, Johnny and Annie sat together on the settee, holding hands and tremulously working out their future.

When the family returned about four o'clock in the morning, they were both asleep, Annie in Johnny's bed upstairs, and Johnny on the bedchair downstairs.

It was the weekend before they had a chance to tell Johnny's mother. They told her together, Johnny taking the lead.

'Mum,' he said, 'we need some help. We've got ourselves in a mess and we don't know the law about getting married.'

Mrs Bookman, who was in the kitchen preparing dinner dropped the saucepan she was just about to fill with water.

'What sort of a mess?' she said. Then, looking at the two strained faces, 'Oh, my God, you're only children your-selves.'

Mr Bookman and Ron were down at the pub. She pulled out a kitchen stool and sat down heavily on it. 'You had better tell me everything. When is it due?'

By the time the others returned, dinner was cooking and the house was quiet. Even the wireless had been turned off, as Mr Bookman commented when he entered. 'Thought you'd gone and left me, ducks,' he said, putting his arm round his wife's waist and swinging her round several times. 'What's the matter?' He looked from one to the other. 'You all look as though you dropped a quid and found a tanner.'

They told him; well, his wife told him. Ron was there too – Annie discovered there were few secrets in this family. A crisis for one was a crisis for them all.

'You bloody young—' but Mrs Bookman intervened. 'It's too late for that sort of talk, Charlie. We have to do what is best now for Johnny and Annie and ... and the baby.'

'What do your parents say about it?' Mr Bookman turned to Annie and she saw tears glinting in his eyes.

'They ... they don't know.' In spite of her efforts she couldn't stop her voice from quivering.

'And they mustn't know,' Mrs Bookman said, looking at her husband. 'Annie's father is still in hospital recovering from a heart attack. He wouldn't be able to stand the shock of news like this.'

'He'll have to know, or her mother will. It'll be up to her whether she tells him or not.'

Mrs Bookman shook her head. 'Poor woman's got enough worry, and from what Annie tells me I doubt if they'd help her much. Although,' she went on, turning to the girl, 'many mothers say they'd turn you out, but when it comes to it they don't.'

'Mummy would.'

Mrs Bookman placed a restraining hand on her husband's arm. 'The way I see it is that we're in the best position to help Johnny and Annie at the moment. Later, when your father is better, Annie, we can have a rethink, but for the present we'll respect both your wishes and keep your secret.'

'You can't keep a thing like this secret.' Charlie Bookman was pacing the tiny room, back and forth, back and forth.

'We have to, if we don't want her father's death on our consciences. Listen, if Annie gets a job away somewhere . . . she has suggested returning to where she was evacuated, but I think that's a bit risky. I hate being deceitful but it is the best thing in this case, I think. Johnny stays here and earns as much as he can, and when Annie can no longer work she returns to have the baby.'

'Maggie, sometimes you take my breath away. There's no room for a baby here.'

'Of course there is,' she replied calmly. 'It won't be for long, and during the time Annie's waiting for the little 'un to arrive Johnny will be looking for a job and a flat. He can do bar-work in the evenings, window-cleaning, there are a lot of odd jobs he can pick up if he searches around. And it won't matter if it's one room to start with, they can go on from there . . .'

Mr Bookman, and Ron too, put forward several more obstacles, but she dismissed them all. 'You can always find a reason why not,' she said quietly, 'but it's the baby you've got to think about now. Poor little mite didn't ask to come into this world, but it's on the way and it's got two parents living, which is more than many have after this last six years. Who are we to deny it that? It's our grandchild too, remember, and if you can't help your own then it's a poor look-out for the rest of humanity. Now if that dinner's finished cooking we'll stop talking about it while we eat. OK?'

'OK,' they all weakly agreed.

Annie didn't think she could eat a thing, but with encouragement from the others she managed to get through.

Afterwards she followed Mrs B, as she had taken to calling her, into the tiny kitchen.

'Let me help, I can't just sit there,' she said.

'Get the cups out then, and bugger the tea ration. I suppose we'll have plenty of the stuff again soon, now the war's over. At least you'll have a peacetime baby, Annie.'

But suddenly Annie couldn't see for the tears rushing from her eyes. Stumbling towards the table she sat down on the bright-red stool and sobbed.

'There, there, there my love, have a good cry and get it out of your system.' Mrs Bookman bent over and comforted her as she might a very young child. When the weeping had subsided she said, 'Listen, Annie, I've just had a wonderful idea. You can go and stay with Auntie Bess in the country.'

'Auntie . . .' the tears were still in her voice and she shuddered them away. 'B-bess?'

'That's right. She's a darling. She's my aunt really – about seventy now but you'd never think it. She was widowed very young and she ran a cat's-meat-shop after-wards. Later, when trade was bad she went to work in one of the big shops in the West End. Smart she was, and with a good brain. Got to be head of her department. Always wore lovely clothes. Anyway, about ten years ago she went to live in the country, little place hiding in the Sussex Downs. Tell you what, Annie, why don't we go and see her. She loves company and she's got a spare bedroom. Be ideal for you until your time comes. We could get you a wedding ring so you won't have no unpleasantness like . . .'

'I don't know . . . and what will I do for money. I really need to keep on with my job for as long as I can. And it would be cheating to have a wedding-ring, wouldn't it?'

'Well now, as the law stands, you can't marry without your parents' consent until you're twenty-one. But you can marry at sixteen with their consent. That poses problems, love, don't it?'

'It would mean I'd have to tell them? I wonder what they'd do? You know, Mrs B, I don't believe they'd allow me to marry.' In her mind she added, 'Johnny' but her tongue stayed silent.

'Are we having a cuppa today or next week, Maggie?' Charlie Bookman popped his head round the kitchen door. 'We're all bloody parched in here, gal.'

'Just coming.' She turned to Annie. 'Think about it, love. You've got nothing to lose by coming to see her, have you now?'

Annie thought of nothing else for the rest of the day and most of that night. She knew she had to make her decision quickly, for Mrs B had told her that she would probably begin to 'show' within weeks. If she told her parents and obtained their consent to marry – but she simply couldn't see that happening. Her mother would disown her, she was in no doubt about that. These last few years had wiped away any lingering dreams that she was anything other than an ornament for her family. A model daughter tucked away to boarding-school to be brought out and paraded now and then. Then there was her father's condition to consider. Would the shock really kill him?

If they couldn't marry yet, surely the best thing would be to accept Aunt Bessie's hospitality until the baby was born. Beyond that her thoughts refused to travel. And it wasn't certain that Aunt Bess would take her in anyway, although Johnny's mum was so confident.

On Monday morning Anita's mother remarked how hollow-eyed she looked. 'Too much celebrating,' she said. 'You look positively *ill*, child. You'd better see the doctor and ask him for a tonic. I can't look after you as well as your father.'

'I'm all right,' she mumbled, 'just tired.'

'I'm not surprised, out every evening. With that boy you brought to the hospital, I suppose. Johnny something or other?' Suddenly a different look appeared on her face and she screwed her eyes up in concentration. 'That's not that schoolboy you were messing around with at Buckingham Palace that time, is it?'

Annie faced her defiantly across the breakfast table. 'Yes,' she said, 'it is, and we want to be married.'

'Married. What nonsense. You're only a child.'

'No mother, I'm not. And you may as well know this too. I'm going to have a baby.'

She gripped the edge of the table and watched a dozen or more expressions roll across her mother's face. At last Mrs Evesham spoke, seeming to have difficulty in getting the words out.

'Anita, did – I hear – you – correctly? Did you say . . .' she swallowed her words, then they came out in a rush, 'did you say a baby?'

'Yes.' The girl lowered her head.

'Are you sure?'

'Yes.'

'Pack your bags. I never want to see you in this house again. And don't try cajoling your father into changing my mind either, because it won't work.'

'Johnny and I want to get married.' Annie's knuckles were white as she increased her hold on the edge of the table. 'We need your permission.'

'*Never.* You did this thing without the blessing of marriage – why bother now? I'm going to my room to lie down. When I come out I want you gone; do you understand?'

'Only too well. But first I shall tell you something. This baby, our baby, Johnny's and mine,' she saw the shiver pass across her mother's features as she said the words, 'will be born into a loving environment whatever material benefits are missing. I *want* Johnny's baby. I'm sorry it's like this – we should have waited, but that too was mostly my fault . . .'

Mrs Evesham clapped her hands over her ears. 'I won't listen to any more. You've broken my heart and I don't wish to know the sordid details. One other thing, Anita. Keep away from your father. It will kill him to know what sort of girl you really are. I'll . . .' For the first time she faltered. 'I'll think of something to explain your absence. I've never lied to him in all our married life, but because of you I shall do so now. I'll – think of something,' she said again, 'because he'll be coming home soon.' Turning away abruptly she left the room and Annie heard her slowly walking upstairs.

CHAPTER 16

1945

Annie heard her mother's bedroom door close, then she went upstairs herself. Taking her suitcase from the top of the wardrobe she methodically emptied the chest of drawers, then moved on to the wardrobe itself. She wondered for how long these clothes would fit, but she would need them after the baby was born.

Last of all she came to the dressing-table with its three mirrors. As she waggled the side ones to look at the back of her hair it released the memory of when her parents had bought the dressing-table for her. She had loved this one as soon as she saw it in the furniture store but her mother thought it too big.

'Whatever do you need three mirrors for? Ridiculous.' She had wandered across to a tiny dressing-table, 'This is nice,' she said, 'and perfectly adequate. After all you'll only be using it during the school holidays.'

She was eight at the time and had been at the boarding-school for a year. Standing perfectly still before the three-mirrored one now she recalled her childish voice saying petulantly, 'I don't like that one, I'd rather go without.'

'Nonsense, child.' Her mother took her arm and turned her away from the one she wanted to the small one. 'This will go very well in your room.' Her father had inclined his head slightly as she went to protest again and then he said, 'Why don't you have a wander round and see what else they have, Anita, while your mother and I discuss the matter.' She knew then that there was just a chance that she might be able to have the one she had set her heart on. Her father didn't often interfere but when he did it was usually on her behalf. She never knew how he did it but when he came and fetched her and they walked through the maze of other furniture to where her mother was waiting for them, he said quietly, 'Remember to thank your mother properly and keep the dressing-table in good order, Anita.' She always had.

She wanted to jump up and kiss him but she knew that that might lose her the precious dressing-table if her mother saw the gesture. She remembered how she had squeezed his hand hard and said squeakily, 'I'm so excited, Daddy. It's beautiful.'

Looking at it again now with that memory so close in her heart the tears cascaded down her cheeks. She laid her hand on the wood and gently stroked it and when she looked up she saw, through her tears, three blurred images in the triple mirrors.

Out of nowhere it seemed another childhood memory surfaced. She was very small, possibly no more than three or four, and she had had earache for most of the day. She woke in the night, screaming with pain, and her mother made up a hot-water bottle and laid it on her pillow to warm it for her. She had cuddled her for a while until the pain eased a bit, before letting the warm pillow send her to sleep. It was the only comfort memory she had of her mother and she clung to it now to stop her hating the woman who had just ordered her out of the house.

At the bedroom door she gave a last look round, then, gently touching Johnny's ring which hung on its chain round her neck permanently now because her fingers had long since grown too big for it, she picked up her suitcase in one hand, her handbag in the other, and walked slowly down the carpeted stairs. There was no sound from her mother's bedroom.

That evening after work she told Mrs B she had left home for good and would like to meet Aunt Bessie at the weekend. Johnny announced that he had two jobs, his daytime one and working in a café at night. 'Tried for a job behind the bar down the road, but my age was against me. But this'll do for a start and you can come in some nights and sit over a cuppa, Annie. That way we'll still see each other.'

'No, Johnny, I shall carry on with my job for as long as I

can and maybe get an evening job myself. That way we shall be able to afford to rent a place of our own, even a small flat.'

Johnny kissed her. 'No, sweetheart. Not an evening job. Carry on with the daytime one a bit longer if you're sure you feel up to it, but no more than that. We'll get by and some day you'll have a house and garden that's worthy of you. We'll be poor for a while, I daresay, but not for ever, Annie, not for ever.'

They were sitting in the cosy room in Johnny's home, his parents having gone for a drink after telling Annie she must stay at least until the weekend and the visit to Aunt Bessie. 'We can take the bedchair up to Johnny's room,' Mrs B said guilelessly. 'I think there's room, then at least you'll be together.'

Johnny was working over the weekend so Mrs Bookman and Annie went together to see Aunt Bessie. They took the train from Victoria to Brighton and the bus from outside the station to Aunt Bessie's village.

Annie thought Aunt Bessie was like a softer version of Johnny's mum. She hugged her and said how much she hoped she would come and stay.

'It's very kind of you,' Annie said.

'It will be lovely for me to have company for a while, too.' Aunt Bessie had a wonderfully wide smile and Annie felt at ease immediately. After a meal the three of them took a stroll round the village, and when they returned Johnny's mum brought up the subject of a wedding-ring.

Annie took a deep breath. 'Mum,' she said, almost

shyly, because only during this last weekend had Mrs Bookman suggested that she began using the word. 'Mum, please don't think I am ungrateful, but Johnny and I have discussed this and we would prefer to wait until I can wear a ring legally. We – we don't want to embarrass you though, but we . . .' she paused aware of both women's eyes intently on her, 'we feel this is best for us.'

'And for the baby?' Mrs Bookman's voice was gentle and questioning.

'We don't know. But if it is necessary we can do it later and in any case we shall marry as soon as ever we can.' Annie reached up and fingered the ring round her neck. 'We love each other, we are committed to each other and a ring won't make any difference to that.'

'That's fair. No, Annie, my love, if you can do it that way I won't interfere.'

It wasn't easy to adjust to living with Johnny's family. They treated her as one of them and couldn't have been kinder or more helpful. She loved them all dearly now but it was so different from living at home, or even with the Dovers in Winchurch.

'You're lucky not having morning sickness,' Mrs Bookman said one day when she and Annie were together in the kitchen. 'Had it with the three of mine – still, it's a small price to pay for a new little life.'

Johnny's mother behaved so naturally with her that sometimes it made her want to cry. This is how life should be, she thought. Maggie Bookman never condemned, never said having Annie in the house made more work and caused inconvenience. She did mention becoming a grand-mother one day, though.

'Didn't ever think young Johnny would be the first to make us grandparents,' she said. 'Well, you wouldn't, would you, not when you have two older sons?'

The whole family rallied round, even Charlie Bookman, after his initial outburst to his son, had been totally accepting of the situation.

It was Charlie who eventually found them somewhere to live. 'It's two rooms in a semi-basement,' he said, 'but there's an indoor lavatory down there, which is more than Maggie and I had when we got wed. Could do with a lick of paint and a bit of tarting up, but I'll see to that for you. That's why the rent's cheap. It's in Lamont Street, over the back there.'

They went to look at the rooms that evening before Johnny went to work. Annie, now five and a half months' pregnant went carefully down the steep steps, behind Johnny, and with his father behind her.

'No chance of you stumbling then, sandwiched between us,' Charlie Bookham said.

He inserted the key and the rusty door creaked as he pushed hard to open it.

'I'll stay out here and have a fag,' he said, getting out his rizlas and tobacco, 'while you two look round.'

'What d'you think, Annie?' Johnny's hand slid into hers.

Annie looked at the two tiny rooms where the hearts-and-flowers patterned paper was peeling from the walls and the ceiling was the colour of sour milk.

She felt more depressed than ever before in her life.

Even with the light on, the room was in semi-darkness. She looked through the smeary window. Gazing upwards she could see ankles and feet as people walked past, while immediately outside her future father-in-law leant against the concrete wall and inhaled deeply on his cigarette.

'It will be a start, Johnny,' she said.

'I know it's not what we had in mind, Annie, but we can make it nice, I'm sure we can.'

She returned the pressure of his squeeze on her hand and, fiercely quelling her doubts, she turned towards him and smiled into his anxious face.

'Our first home, Johnny. We've got years ahead of us to work and save and improve our lot.'

'And we will,' he said, kissing her, 'we will, Annie, that's a promise.'

There was a small grate in one room and a very old gas-stove next to the deep yellowy butler sink in the other. They settled the deal with the landlord, Charlie Bookman paying a week's rent as a deposit to hold the rooms.

'Gives me a chance to decorate,' he said. 'Maggie'll help with curtains and cushions and I reckon as to how she'll let you have a couple of chairs too – clear our place out a bit and give us more room.'

In bed that night in Johnny's room back in his home, Annie thought fleetingly of her old bedroom and of the one in the Dovers' house.

Now she was in his bed and he was in the bedchair. As she looked down on him as he lay fast asleep an overwhelming rush of love shot through her whole being. 'It won't be for long, Johnny darling,' she murmured. 'Once the baby is born we'll get on our feet and some day we'll have that shop and our own house and garden.' As the child kicked inside her she winced and laid her hands across her stomach.

CHAPTER 17

Annie and Johnny moved into Lamont Street two weeks later. True to his word Charlie Bookman had lightened the place with some cream-coloured paint he got from a friend who had had it stored since before the war. His wife had put up some net curtains at the little window that afforded the glimpses of the lower half of people walking along the pavement.

'Later, I'll dye our blackout curtains if I can,' she said. 'They'll be warmer in the winter and we ought ter be able to do them bottle-green or a darkish blue if I bleach 'em first. Doubt if we'll get em lighter than that but they'll keep the draughts out.'

She and her daughter-in-law, Doris, also scrubbed the floors and black-leaded the grate until it shone. They refused to let Annie do any of this. 'You've got to think of the baby, and anyway we're more used to it than you,' Maggie said. Annie couldn't take offence at that because she knew it was true. On her own she would not have known where to begin, but she insisted she could clean the sink and stove, and set to with a will.

Annie was thankful she still had her job, because, apart from the money she earned, it got her out of those poky rooms for most of the day.

In August the Allies dropped the first atomic bombs on Hiroshima and Nagaski and a week later, on 14 August the war with Japan finished. The next day, 15 August, became a public holiday to be known as VJ Day (Victory in Japan).

They both went to work as usual, only to return after a while, fighting their way home with thousands of others, who did not realize that this was to be a public holiday. It had been announced at almost midnight and again on the early-morning news, but as Annie and Johnny didn't possess a wireless set they didn't know. Neither had any desire to go out celebrating but later in the day they went round to Johnny's parents for a few hours.

'Doris has gone to her mum's,' Maggie Bookman said. 'Now she'll be counting the days 'til Jim gets home. It was written all over her face.'

'It could be some time, duck,' Charlie said, 'but reckon we'll all be glad to see 'im back.'

About five o'clock Johnny said he was going to his evening job in the café, 'Because this morning the boss said that so many places will be closed it'll mean we'll do good business. He's promised me double pay if I work tonight until the revellers have gone home, Annie. You'll be all right, won't you? And we do need the money, my darling.'

'Of course, Johnny. I'll be fine. I've an interesting book and I'll probably have an early night. Got your key?'

'Yes. You could go round to mum and dad's if you get lonely. Don't think they're going out. Mum said she'd celebrated in May, but I think Doris's family are going to a knees-up.' He kissed her lingeringly. 'I'll come in quietly, 'case you're asleep.'

During the evening she heard and saw the revellers along the street, and memories of VE night when she and Johnny went up to Trafalgar Square returned. Sighing deeply she patted her stomach and thought, I want this baby, more than anything I want Johnny's child, but I wish we had waited. That it didn't have to be like this, with no money, a tumbledown place in a poor area to live, and no prospects for the immediate future.

She wouldn't burden Johnny with these sombre thoughts, but she privately faced the knowledge that life was going to be a struggle for a long, long time.

All was quiet outside when she went to bed. Obviously most of the revellers had gone up West, and with a deep sigh she pulled the thin sheet over herself and closed her eyes. She tried to imagine what it would be like and how she would manage when she had a baby to put in the basket crib Maggie Bookman had lovingly restored and given to her.

A noise woke her sometime around midnight and she became aware that there were people in the basement area outside. They were obviously drunk, and were singing and shouting obscenities. Lying very still she wished Johnny were home with her. Although perhaps not, she thought, for he would surely want to go out and tackle them. One thing; it was a sturdy door and it was locked so they couldn't get in unless they broke a window. The laughter and loud voices continued for a while, and she thought she heard the flap on the letter-box slap into place. Suddenly there was more shouting and what sounded like a stampede up the area steps. She held her breath and an enormous bang made her clutch her stomach as she rolled out of bed and found herself doubled up on the floor. Her last thought as she lost consciousness was that it was a bomb and she was buried beneath the debris of the café near the Palladium and she couldn't find Johnny or his mum.

When Annie came to she was cradled in Johnny's arms in an unfamiliar room.

'Johnny, what happened? Was it – was it a bomb. Is the war not over after all?'

'It's all right, Annie. You're fine, you weren't injured, thank God. No, not a bomb, a bloody firework some idiots pushed through the letterbox.'

'Here's Edie,' someone said, 'good as a doctor is Edie. She knows what it's all about. Let her have a look at you, duck. You've 'ad a bit of a shock.'

Edie felt her all over, looked at her tongue and deeply into her eyes, asked if she felt any pains, then declared her to be 'None the worse for it all,' patted her hand and left.

'She's a good 'un, is Edie,' someone said. 'Now, 'ave you two youngsters got anywhere ter go ternight, 'cos that place ain't 'abitable now.'

'Yes,' Johnny said quickly, 'we can go to my mum's. It's not far. Come on, Annie, reckon you can manage?'

He helped her to her feet. 'Thanks,' he said to the neighbours in whose house they were.

'Yes, thank you,' Annie said, 'we're very grateful.' She saw the strange looks they gave her as she and Johnny walked towards the door.

The Bookmans took it all in their stride when they were woken in the early hours of the morning by Johnny and Annie, and at three a.m. they were sitting drinking tea and listening to how Johnny arrived home from work to see half a dozen drunken lads coming up the area steps from his house.

'Within seconds there was this explosion,' he said, 'I pushed me elbow through the window and climbed in to find Annie in a heap on the floor and the place on fire.

'It's in a bit of a mess,' he said. 'Everyone sloshing water all over the place, but it put the fire out and I'll go round tomorrer and sort it out.'

'The baby's still kicking though,' Annie said.

'Thank God. You take it easy now, Annie, and let us take care of you for a while,' Mrs Bookman said. Suddenly she noticed Johnny's arm.

'You're hurt, son,' she said. 'Here, let me look.' It was quite a deep cut he had sustained when he took more glass out to get Annie through the window.

'Couldn't get out the door,' he said, 'it was on fire. Don't fuss Mum, it's nothing much – I wrapped me hankie round it when I went back to help them. Dipped it in the water and tied it up. That soon stopped the bleeding.'

Mrs Bookman cleaned the wound and Annie felt guilty that while everyone was making sure she and the baby were not injured Johnny had been and she hadn't even noticed. They slept in each other's arms in Johnny's bed for what was left of the night.

It was nearly a week before they could return to the basement flat, after Charlie Bookman had helped his son get it shipshape again and Annie promised herself that once the child was born and she could walk and run again instead of waddle everywhere, she would sort something out about finding somewhere better for them to live.

She dreamt one night that they were in Bushton, by the river, and had their own little business with a row of boats for hire ... Why not? she thought, when she woke and it was still vivid in her mind. We both liked it there and now the war's over people will be wanting holidays. If Johnny can find work there for a while, one day it could be more than a dream.

Annie carried on with her job until a week before the baby was due. Then, enveloped in one of the pretty smocks Johnny's mum had made for her and with a suitcase filled with nappies, matinée jackets, tiny wrapover vests and nightgowns, bootees and little romper-suits she left London for the Sussex village and Aunt Bessie. The case had been presented to her a few days before and was a gift from them all. The entire family had been knitting and sewing to give this first grandchild his or her layette. Annie herself had knitted a couple of tiny garments, under Mrs B's guidance, and felt proud of her efforts. All her life, if they had needed something they had gone to a shop and bought it, but Johnny's family almost always made it themselves, even unravelling old garments, putting the wool into skeins to be washed, before winding it into balls for re-using. Annie had never done anything like that before and at first didn't know what Johnny's mum was talking about when she said, 'Hold your hands out for five minutes, love, so I can undo this jumper.'

Mrs Bookman was a fast worker and Annie marvelled as the knitted rows of the old garment were wound round her outstretched hands at a terrific speed.

'It's all crinkly,' she said, 'won't it look funny?'

'Bless you, no Annie. Once it's washed and dried it will knit up a treat. Nice soft wool this and as it's lemon it'll do for a boy or a girl.'

Johnny went with her on the Sunday morning, returning in time to get to his evening job. 'There's no need,' she said. 'We could save the fare because it isn't as though you can stop long.'

'Poo, bloody poo,' he said, 'you don't think I'll let you go alone, do you?' Laughing, she hugged him. 'I expect someone would have insisted on coming, but I'm glad it's you, Johnny. I'll miss you, you know.'

'I jolly well hope so. Aunt Bessie's got a phone so I'll be able to talk to you. Can ring from the box on the corner. You're not scared, are you, gal?'

She shook her head. 'No, well, not much. A little, if I'm honest. But your mum says the pain is one you forget quickly. It's not like an illness. Once the baby's out the worst pain is over, that's what she said.'

They were silent for a few moments, then, her voice quiet, she said, 'In a while, maybe a few months, I'd like to tell my father he's a grandad. I thought I could telephone the hospital after the baby's born to see how he is, and maybe talk to the doctor about his condition. He's going on fine and should be going home soon. I don't know what my mother is going to tell him to account for my absence but once I know he's better I'd like him to know about us and about our baby.'

Johnny kissed her. 'After we're married. That's the time I reckon. Then you can tell him you're married to me and we now have a child. He will be welcome in our home, wherever it is, Annie, any time. He's a real gentleman. Remember when you introduced us outside Buckingham Palace that day, he shook my hand. But your mother will not be welcome, Annie. I'll never forgive her for the way she's treated you. If you ever want to see her it'll have to be without me. To turn you out like that . . .' His eyes flashed, cold as steel, and then suddenly he said, 'What on earth are we doing, reviving old scores? We're on the way to being a real family, Annie, you, me and the bump.' Gently he touched her stomach. 'Won't be long now gal – remember you said once you were glad you weren't a man, well I'll tell you this for nothing, I'm very glad I'm not a woman.'

She smiled at him, then became serious again as she returned to her theme.

'If they won't let us marry until I'm twenty-one, Johnny, it will be five years and I'd like my dad to know before then.'

He thumped his head dramatically with his hand, ' 'Course you would, and we'll tell him, just as soon as it's safe to. When the doc says we can, how about that?'

'Mmm. All right.'

'Listen Annie, I've bin wanting to say this but didn't know how. I know we said we wouldn't 'cos it seems like cheating, but – well, I've thought about it all a lot lately and I've changed me mind. I'll marry you prop'ly, in a church, just as soon as it's possible. Meanwhile,' he fumbled in his pocket and brought out a small, white leather pouch, 'you don't have to wear it if you don't want to. . . .'

She took the gold band from its soft casing, her thumping heart suddenly still. 'Oh, Johnny. Yes, of course I'll wear it.'

'You don't mind – that I had second thoughts, like. See, I don't want anyone saying things about you Annie, specially when I'm not there to protect you.'

She swallowed hard, more ashamed than ever before in her life, of what she had thought he was about to say,about changing his mind. Blinking away the tears that threatened she handed the plain gold band to him.

'Here, will you – will you say the words?'

Awkwardly he took her hand. 'With this ring. . . .'

That night, by her single bed in Aunt Bessie's pretty spare room Annie knelt and prayed for her family. Johnny, her father, Johnny's mum and dad and his brothers and sister-in-law, for Aunt Bessie who had welcomed her into her home, and lastly for her mother, that somehow she might find peace, because Annie knew already that there was no way that she could abandon the child now kicking inside her, the child that was the result of their love for each other.

Annie's labour began early one morning, a little after six, and by ten o'clock Bessie had called the midwife. Between them they massaged her back and tried to keep her

comfortable. She spoke to Johnny at midday when he telephoned during his lunch break. She tried to sound cheerful and confident but it wasn't easy. A huge pain caught
her as they said their farewells and she was sweating as
Aunt Bessie took the phone from her and told Johnny not
to worry, everything was going well.

She tried to do what she was told, puff and push in the
right places, and she hung on to Aunt Bessie's hand with
such force that the poor woman was forced to cry out
herself. Just when she thought she couldn't do it an excru-
ciating pain almost made her pass out and dimly, she
heard the midwife say, 'Good girl, one more, come on,
you're nearly there.' She could hear herself screaming now,
then suddenly it was all over, and the midwife was saying,
'Well done, Annie, you have a beautiful baby boy.'

Suddenly she felt herself going, heard the anxious voices
and realized with horror that the baby hadn't cried. That
was when she did pass out.

Annie opened her eyes to find Aunt Bessie still beside her.

From a great distance she heard her own voice say, 'He's
dead, isn't he? My son was stillborn.'

Bessie's arm was supporting her as she said quietly, 'No
Annie. He's alive and well.'

'But – but he didn't cry and you were all bothered and—'

'He only needed a slap to get his breath. He has a powerful voice I can tell you. It was you who needed the attention for a few moments my love. You fainted on us.'

Aunt Bessie eased her up in the bed and the midwife
gently placed the baby in her arms. He seemed to be
making little chuckling sounds and he looked like a minia-

ture Johnny.

'Oh,' she whispered, holding the fragile bundle to her breast, 'you are so beautiful.'

'I'll make you a cup of tea,' Aunt Bessie said, 'then you can have a good long sleep and be fresh for when Johnny comes down this evening. You can stay here as long as you need, you know, Annie, and when you are back in town I hope you'll often come for weekends and holidays in the country. I should like that and I'll be able to see more of this little fellow too.'

Aunt Bessie touched the baby's downy head gently.

'We will, Aunt Bessie. And I'll never forget your kindness, never.'

'Don't be silly, you're keeping the room aired for me, aren't you?'

She turned when she reached the door. 'Ben and I couldn't have children, you know, it was the only thing missing in our marriage. We both wanted them.'

Quietly she slipped from the room and Annie looked at her baby son's dimpled hands and perfect nails. A tear fell on to his soft skin as she kissed his forehead.

'That'll be them now, Annie,' Bessie said when the doorbell rang that evening. 'I bet Maggie will be the proudest grandma in London.'

Annie gazed at her baby son. She looked radiant. Johnny came in alone.

'You all right, Annie?' He kissed her tenderly and laid a huge bunch of bronze and yellow chrysanthemums on the bed.

'I'm fine, darling.'

He gazed at her adoringly and gently took hold of her hand.

'Don't you want to see the baby?' she said.

Almost shyly Johnny looked at his son. 'He's a funny-looking blighter, isn't he, Annie?'

She smiled. 'He'll do all right, Johnny, I'm sure he will. Your mum has promised to help me, and we'll make up to him in love what he hasn't got in money.'

'You bet we will.' Johnny bent over the tiny head cradled in her arms. 'Tell you something, Annie, he's already the luckiest little chap alive except for me, because he has you as his mum.'